THE FOUR DIFFERENT PETALS

Coming in light

Varun Ramesh

Copyright © Varun Ramesh 2025
All Rights Reserved.

ISBN
Paperback 979-8-89929-337-5
Hardcase 979-8-89929-321-4

This book has been published with all efforts taken to make the material error-free after the consent of the author. However, the author and the publisher do not assume and hereby disclaim any liability to any party for any loss, damage, or disruption caused by errors or omissions, whether such errors or omissions result from negligence, accident, or any other cause.

While every effort has been made to avoid any mistake or omission, this publication is being sold on the condition and understanding that neither the author nor the publishers or printers would be liable in any manner to any person by reason of any mistake or omission in this publication or for any action taken or omitted to be taken or advice rendered or accepted on the basis of this work. For any defect in printing or binding the publishers will be liable only to replace the defective copy by another copy of this work then available.

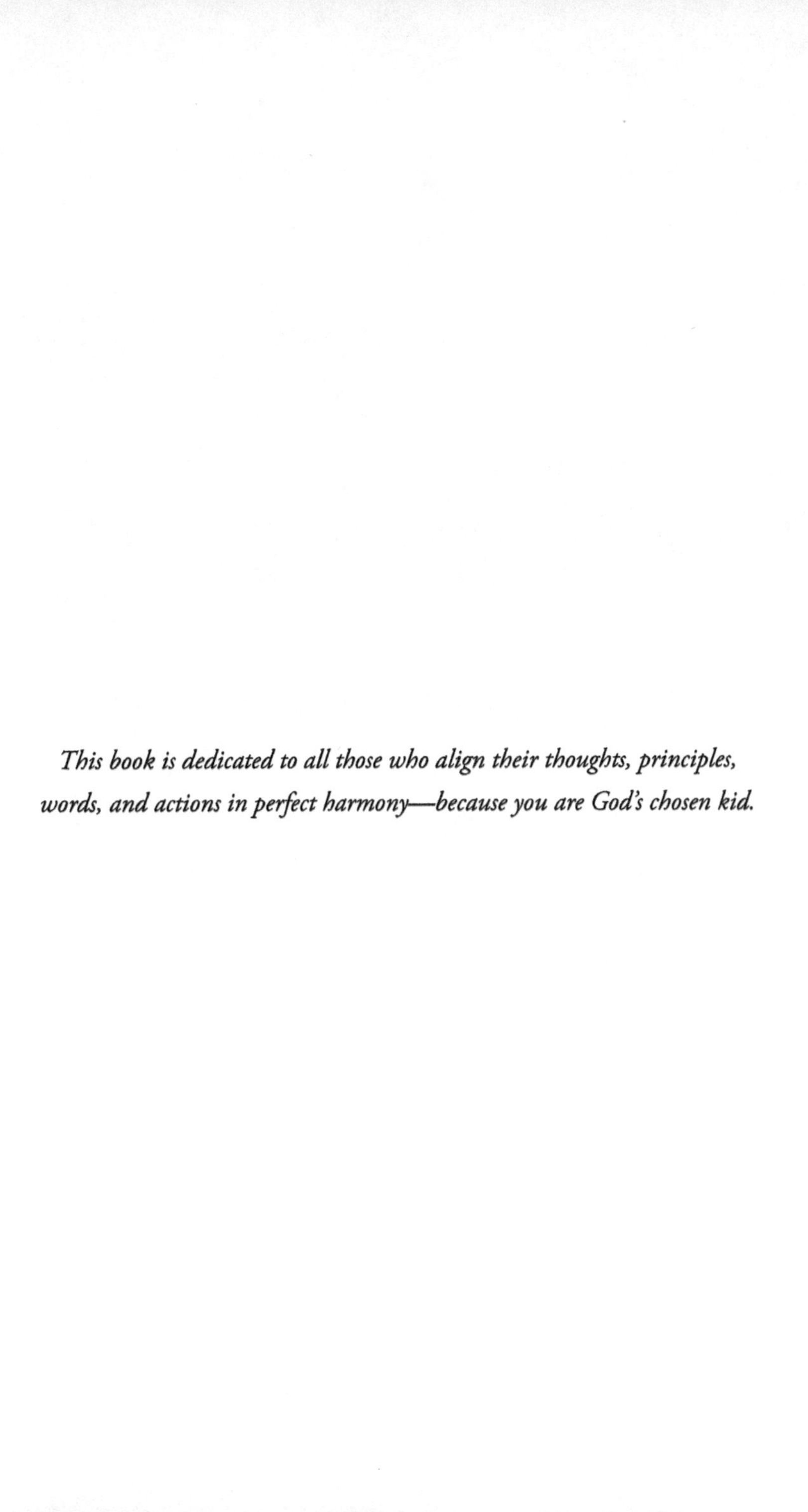

This book is dedicated to all those who align their thoughts, principles, words, and actions in perfect harmony—because you are God's chosen kid.

Contents

Chapter One

"Raindrops of Honour"

In the bustling city of Bangalore, where dreams and aspirations blended with the relentless rain, Atharva, a hero in his own right, stepped out of the airport into the chaotic symphony of honking horns and splashing raindrops.

Dressed in crisp formals, he sought shelter under the flickering airport lights and raised his hand to hail a cab.

As the rain poured mercilessly, a worn-out cab screeched to a halt in front of Atharva.

He climbed into the vehicle, only to realise that the rain had invaded every inch of the cab, transforming it into a makeshift pond. Determined, Atharva smiled and decided to weather the storm.

As the cab manoeuvred through the flooded streets, the water level inside rose steadily. Atharva, undeterred.

The cab driver, sensing the discomfort, offered a fresh pair of shirt and socks, revealing a genuine kindness in his eyes.

"These were meant for my son's birthday. He's in college, aspiring to join the Air Force. I wish I could provide more for him," the cab driver confessed.

Without uttering a word, Atharva accepted the shirt and socks and wore them, acknowledging the unspoken bond formed in that dilapidated cab.

Little did he know, the gesture would weave a story of resilience and honour.

In another corner of the city, the cab driver's son, Shiru, faced ridicule and humiliation in college.

His peers, blinded by materialism, belittled him for his father's occupation.

But Shiru remained silent, fuelled by the values instilled in him by his cab-driving father.

As the cab approached a flyover, the driver realised he had taken the wrong route. Unfazed, Atharva took charge, declaring that he would find the location on foot.

However, the relentless rain had caused a communication blackout, leaving them without the means to pay for the ride.

With a sense of responsibility, Atharva guided the cab driver to a hidden arch where he could find an ATM.

Atharva requested the driver to stay put, reassuring him that he would return within five minutes.

Under the shelter of the arch, Atharva enlisted the help of passersby to shield himself from the rain.

As the minutes ticked by, he emerged from the shadowy background, fully dressed in the regalia of an Air Vice Marshal.

With an air of commanding authority and respect, the Air Vice Marshal's eyes gleamed with the fierce intensity of an eagle.

His presence was palpable; his uniform was a testament to his dedication and strength. Every passerby felt compelled to give him their full attention and unwavering respect.

Air Vice Marshal Atharva thanked the cab driver for the shirt and socks. However, the tranquillity was disrupted by a security lapse.

Atharva took the cab driver to his son's college, and as Atharva made his entrance, Air Force Marshals arrived on campus.

Encountering the sight of Air Force Officer Atharva being saluted by his peers beside him, an ununiformed cab driver gazed in awe, a look of disbelief and wonderment in his eyes, questioning the reality of the scene before him.

The students couldn't help but stare at the officer, admiring his uniform adorned with medals.

Shiru was there, and his eyes widened in surprise at the sight of the officer standing beside his father.

Atharva approached Shiru and, with a warm smile, offered words of encouragement and a life lesson line: "Your father may be monetarily poor, but he is rich in ethics and honesty.

In the next ten years, honesty will be the most lucrative skill you possess."

To top it off, he wished Shiru a heartfelt happy birthday.

As the rain continued to fall, the city witnessed the convergence of two worlds—one driven by materialism and the other fortified by values and integrity.

In the end, the raindrops of honour prevailed over the superficial judgements, leaving behind a tale of resilience, kindness, and the enduring power of principles.

♥

Dear Readers,

Allow me to introduce myself. I am Varun Ramesh, the fictional storyteller and author of the book you are about to embark on, "The Four Different Petals." As I extend my gratitude for your interest in buying Atharva's Journey.

My path has been marked by numerous endeavours, from pursuing a degree in engineering to exploring the realms of law, attempting the challenges of UPSC, trying my hand at lecturing, venturing into business, and even delving into the complexities of risk analysis at International Exchange (Clearing House). Each of these experiences has contributed to the fabric of my understanding and the perspective with which I approach life.

However, the idea of this book, the seeds of "The Four Different Petals," were sown a decade ago. At that time, I lacked the maturity and insight required to articulate the story I envisioned. Today, after countless failures and the invaluable lessons they brought, I find myself standing on the precipice of fulfilling a long-cherished dream.

I chose to break the traditional barrier of an author's introduction, not to entice you to purchase this book. Instead, my intention is to convey that while money can be earned, the time you invest in reading these pages is irreplaceable. This book is not just a literary endeavour for me; it is a vessel carrying a noble inspiration, a message I hope resonates with the next generation.

As you turn the pages, immerse yourself in the world of Atharva. May this narrative serve as a guiding light, encouraging you to navigate the complexities of life with integrity and purpose.

Thank you for joining me on this journey, and may the words within these pages leave a lasting imprint on your heart.

With ♥ & gratitude,

Varun Ramesh

The rain had finally subsided, leaving the city washed and glistening under the streetlights.

Air Vice Marshal Atharva sat back in his office, a mix of exhaustion and satisfaction settling upon him.

The day's duties, missions, and responsibilities were fulfilled, but as the silence of the night enveloped him, Atharva found himself lost in introspection.

Leaning back in his chair, he stared out of the window at the city below, the same city that had witnessed his journey to the pinnacle of the Air Force.

The hum of the city below seemed distant, and in that moment of quiet reflection, Atharva began to recollect the steps that had brought him here.

His mind wandered back to the decision to go to school, a choice that seemed to shape his destiny.

The rain had not only cleansed the city but also acted as a metaphor for the cleansing process Atharva underwent in his reflections.

Life wasn't a linear equation with predefined solutions but a complex, evolving narrative filled with twists and turns.

As he closed his eyes, a sense of gratitude washed over Atharva—gratitude for the challenges, the victories, and the unwavering spirit that had propelled him forward.

The raindrops that had accompanied him throughout his life seemed to whisper a gentle reminder—honour, resilience, and the enduring power of values were the guiding lights that had led him to this very moment.

With a deep breath, Atharva prepared to face the next chapter, uncertain yet determined, knowing that the journey was far from over.

♥

Chapter Two

The soul of the violin

Atharva found himself gradually drifting into a doze, lulled by the rhythmic hum of the fan in his chair. As his consciousness slipped into the realm of dreams, an extraordinary scenario unfolded before him.

In this dream world, he discovered himself in a state of afterlife, surrounded by a surreal classroom setting.

To his astonishment, the classroom was filled with familiar faces from every chapter of his life. People beckoned him to join them, inviting him to sit beside them.

Overwhelmed, he chose an empty table, only to find others gravitating towards him, extending warm welcomes.

Among the attendees was a striking revelation: his oldest friends appeared youthful, defying the passage of time.

Suddenly, a captivating girl entered the classroom, draped in a blue saree.

As the room fell silent, a wave of stillness washed over the air as if the universe itself had paused to honour her presence. Atharva's breath caught, his heart pounding in a rhythm only she could awaken. He turned slowly, his gaze drawn to her as if by an invisible force.

And there she was.

Time seemed to collapse as memories flooded his mind—her laughter, her voice, her warmth—every fragment of the love he thought had been left behind. It was her. Gayathri Shruthi.

His first love.

In that moment, the world around him disappeared. He was no longer the accomplished Air Vice Marshal or the man shaped by trials and triumphs.

He was just a young boy again, standing in the glow of her light, feeling the pure, untainted love that had once defined his entire existence.

The years they'd spent apart melted into insignificance as his eyes met hers.

He saw a reflection of the same wonder, the same tenderness he had carried in his heart all this time.

To his surprise, she took on the role of his first teacher, instigating a whirlwind of emotions within him.

Conflicted, Atharva grappled with the reasons for her presence. In a moment of introspection, he admitted that he hadn't been there when she needed him.

Closing his eyes, Atharva embarked on a journey through his memories. He vividly recalled a rainy day from his childhood when he stood with his family, captivated by the allure of a watch in a street market.

However, his mother accepted the request of taking him to cinema, navigating through the dimly lit corridors to find a movie titled 'Gayathri Shruthi'.

In the darkness of the cinema, he noticed a young girl with enchanting eyes, rosy cheeks, and oiled hair - Gayathri Shruthi.

Though she attended the same school, Atharva had never truly seen her beauty before. As school commenced, he discreetly admired her in the corridors, never mustering the courage to make his presence known.

Unbeknownst to Gayathri Shruthi, he observed her with fascination, even noticing a tiny pimple on her cheek.

As the haunting melody of the Bombay movie song filled the air, Atharva found himself completely entranced.

The music seemed to wrap around him like a warm embrace, pulling him closer to its captivating rhythm.

He couldn't resist the urge to immerse himself in its enchanting notes, moving closer to the source of the sound where the rehearsal team had set up their equipment.

His heart beat with a strange anticipation as he stood near the speaker, feeling the vibrations of the music coursing through him. And then, like a sudden burst of sunlight on a cloudy day, he heard her name, her voice ringing out like a beautiful symphony in the chaos of the dance practice.

"Gayathri... Gayathri Shruthi..."

Instantly, Atharva's gaze darted towards the stage, scanning every face in search of her. But as he looked, a sense of longing began to tug at his heartstrings, for she was nowhere to be found.

Panic threatened to overwhelm him until, slowly, a figure rose from among the dancers, turning towards him with a small smile playing on her lips.

In that moment, time seemed to stand still as Atharva found himself completely captivated by her presence. It was as if the world around him faded into insignificance, leaving only her standing there, her eyes sparkling with an undefinable allure.

A rush of emotions flooded through him, leaving him breathless and bewildered. Could this be love? The thought both thrilled and terrified him, sending his mind into a whirlwind of uncertainty.

He wrestled with his conflicting feelings, wondering if it was even possible to fall for someone in the confines of a school environment.

Fears and doubts gnawed at the edges of his consciousness, threatening to overshadow the euphoria he felt in her presence.

What if his parents found out? What if the school authorities intervened? The mere thought of the repercussions sent a chill down his spine, but he couldn't deny the overwhelming attraction he felt towards her.

And so, despite the fear and uncertainty that plagued his mind, Atharva made a conscious decision to embrace the moment.

He allowed himself to bask in the warmth of her smile, the grace of her movements, and the sheer beauty of her presence while practising for dance.

For now, he would cast aside his worries and revel in the magic of their connection, even if it meant risking everything for the chance of love.

♥

The energy of sports day practice filled the air. Atharva, however, found himself seated in the pavilion, engrossed in a conversation with his friends.

Amidst their chatter, a sudden commotion broke out as a girl emerged, holding a vibrant red flag aloft with determination.

Atharva's gaze followed her movements, and he murmured to his friend, "Oh, she's the sports captain."

His friend, with a touch of loudness, added, "She's our math teacher's daughter. That's how she got the role."

Atharva's heart sank as the realisation hit him like a tonne of bricks. The girl he had been enamoured with, the one he had been secretly admiring, was the daughter of his own teacher.

Fear gripped him as he contemplated the consequences of his feelings for her. The spectre of punishment loomed large – the dreaded possibility of facing a bigger disciplinary action on him.

As the practice concluded and students gathered around the taps to clean up, Atharva found himself coincidentally standing next to her.

In the midst of the bustling activity, their paths crossed, and he accidentally bumped into her, causing their heads to collide. "Sorry," she said softly, her voice barely audible above the din.

Her gentle apology sent a wave of warmth through Atharva's heart, and as she walked away, his gaze lingered on her figure until she disappeared from sight, descending the stairs.

Despite the barriers that stood between them, Atharva couldn't shake the longing he felt for her. With each step she took, his heart followed, yearning for a connection that seemed impossible in the face of societal norms.

♥

As the summer sun beat down, Atharva and his neighbourhood friends found solace in the game of cricket, played on the narrow streets with makeshift wickets.

Amidst the laughter and banter, tensions simmered as blame was passed around for the previous match's loss.

Raghu, a friend and fellow schoolmate of Atharva, took offence at being blamed and retaliated with teasing remarks about each other's school weaknesses.

Hours passed, but the heat of the argument refused to dissipate.

Suddenly, a group of girls on bicycles passed by, one of them catching Atharva's eye – it was Gayathri Shruthi,

Excitedly, Atharva pointed her out to his friends, but Raghu overheard and seized the opportunity to tease Atharva about his apparent fondness for Gayathri.

The teasing escalated as Gayathri made subsequent rounds on her bicycle, with Atharva feeling increasingly frustrated by Raghu's taunts.

The cycle of teasing continued the next day, with the boys becoming louder and Gayathri becoming more uncomfortable with the attention.

On one particular day, Gayathri brought her elder sister along, who, upon witnessing the boys' behaviour, confronted them fiercely.

Atharva, feeling embarrassed and misunderstood, tried to explain himself, but the damage had been done.

The neighbourhood rallied behind Gayathri and her sister, issuing warnings against any further eve-teasing.

In the aftermath, the once lively streets fell silent, devoid of the joyous shouts of cricket.

Atharva and his friends, chastened by the incident, resumed their games quietly, with fewer participants and subdued spirits.

Meanwhile, Gayathri and her friends continued their cycling routine, unaware of the turmoil they had unwittingly caused.

Days passed, and Atharva found himself walking home alone, the weight of guilt and fear heavy on his shoulders.

Suddenly, a familiar voice pierced the silence – Gayathri's. Startled, Atharva turned to see her cycling towards him, alone this time.

♥

His heart raced as she apologised for her sister's actions, her sincerity evident in her eyes.

Atharva, overwhelmed by a mix of emotions, could only manage a feeble response before she sped off, leaving him to grapple with his feelings of remorse and longing.

Unbeknownst to Atharva, Gayathri had been grappling with her own emotions, her curiosity about him growing with each teasing remark.

As she pedalled away, her cheeks flushed with embarrassment, she couldn't help but wonder about the boy named Atharva, who had inadvertently captured her attention.

And so, amidst the backdrop of societal expectations and misunderstandings, the unspoken connection between Atharva and Gayathri continued to blossom, each yearning for a chance to understand the other's heart.

♥

The very next day, as Atharva wandered through the ancient streets of Hampi, being forced to visit his grandparents' house, the memories of Gayathri Shruthi lingered in his mind like a haunting melody.

The vibrant colours of the heritage town, filled with curious foreigners and echoes of history, seemed to blur into the background as his thoughts drifted to her.

Caught in a whirlwind of emotions, Atharva found himself yearning to see her smile once more, to unravel the mysteries of their unspoken connection.

But amidst the cacophony of doubts and uncertainties, he couldn't shake the feeling of guilt for allowing himself to fall so deeply in love. Despite his inner turmoil, Atharva found solace in the warm embrace of his grandparents, the tranquillity of their home providing a temporary respite from the chaos of his emotions.

♥

Yet, as the days passed and his return to school loomed closer, he couldn't help but feel a pang of insecurity about his tanned complexion, a souvenir from his time spent under the scorching sun of Hampi.

Finally back in his neighbourhood, Atharva's anticipation grew as he awaited the familiar sight of Gayathri's presence.

But to his dismay, he learned that she had been absent for a week, a void left by an unexpected incident.

It was revealed that a friend from outside the neighbourhood, named Malum, had boldly declared his affections for Gayathri, and to Atharva's shock, she had accepted his proposal.

The news hit Atharva like a sledgehammer, shattering his hopes and dreams in an instant.

In the wake of this revelation, Atharva found himself adrift in a sea of heartbreak and confusion.

The once familiar melody of the Bombay movie song that had once brought him comfort now served as a painful reminder of the love he had lost.

With a heavy heart, Atharva retreated into the solitude of his home, the background hum of the tape recorder a haunting echo of his shattered dreams.

Exhausted and defeated, he lacked the strength to stand by the speaker and let the music wash over him, leaving him to grapple with the bitter sting of unrequited love.

In the quiet halls of the school, Atharva returned with a subdued air, carrying the weight of his summer adventures hidden within him.

He chose not to divulge the tales of his vacation, preferring instead to keep them close to his heart.

As the morning assembly commenced and prayers began, he felt a gaze upon him, a sensation that drew him to turn around.

There she was, her smile radiant as she caught his eye before swiftly turning away, leaving him to ponder the meaning behind her gaze.

Determined to focus on his studies as he approached his academic year, Atharva navigated the routine of school life.

Yet, amidst the mundane tasks of shoe polish and nail checks, a moment of unexpected connection occurred.

As Gayathri Shruthi, the leader in charge of nail inspections, reached out to examine his hand, their fingers brushed in a fleeting touch that sparked something within both of them.

In that simple interaction, a thread of attraction wove between them, leaving them both with a lingering smile.

Unbeknownst to Atharva, Gayathri found herself drawn to him, stealing moments to watch him from afar, her heart swelling with affection.

When Gayathri saw him in the hallways at school, her heart would race.

She felt a mix of excitement and nervousness, trying to catch his eye while simultaneously hoping she wouldn't trip over her own feet.

The thrill of accidentally brushing hands or sharing a smile was enough to make her cheeks flush with warmth.

She'd daydream about their future together, doodling his name in her notebooks and imagining all the adventures they would have.

Yet, there was always a sense of vulnerability and uncertainty, wondering if he felt the same way, if he thought about her as much as she thought about him.

Friends played a crucial role, too. She'd spend hours dissecting every interaction with her best friends, analysing every word and gesture, seeking advice and reassurance.

And though Atharva remained unaware of her silent admiration, fate had plans to bring them closer together.

♥

One afternoon during the lunch break, as Atharva sought solace in the shade of the ground floor balcony, fate intervened in a playful twist.

A chalk sailed through the air, catching Atharva by surprise, as it landed perfectly in his shirt pocket.

Bewildered, he looked up to see Gayathri, her laughter dancing in her eyes as she repeated the gesture, sending another chalk sailing his way.

As word of this playful exchange spread, whispers of Atharva and Gayathri's connection echoed through the halls.

With each passing day, their bond grew stronger, fuelled by shared glances and stolen moments.

When Atharva finally shared the story of their encounters with his friends, the school erupted into chants of his name whenever Gayathri appeared, their affectionate teasing bringing laughter and warmth to their budding romance.

With each nail inspection, Atharva found himself eagerly awaiting Gayathri's touch, a simple gesture that spoke volumes of their unspoken connection.

And as they navigated the challenges of school life together, their love blossomed, fuelled by the laughter and camaraderie that surrounded them.

In the quaint town where Atharva and Raghu lived, their friendship blossomed amidst the struggles of academic life.

Both known as the underdogs in their school, they found solace in each other's company, especially during their remedial tuition classes.

However, their true adventures began when they decided to ditch tuition and indulge in games of Counter-Strike at the local cybercafé.

It was Raghu who introduced Atharva to the colourful world of Orkut, a social networking platform where friendships med and conversations flowed.

Intrigued by the concept, Atharva allowed Raghu to create an account for him, christening it with the password "AtharvaGayathriShruthi," a playful nod to the girl Atharva often found himself glancing at in school.

As they scrolled through profiles and exchanged banter, Raghu couldn't resist the temptation to play matchmaker.

With mischievous glee, he sent a friend request to Gayathri on behalf of Atharva, using a profile picture of a ruggedly handsome man with six-pack abs.

Atharva watched in both amusement and horror as Raghu executed his plan. Days passed, and to their surprise, Gayathri accepted the friend request, sparking a flurry of excitement between the two friends.

But it was when she sent a hello message along with a message that things took an unexpected turn.

Raghu, seizing the opportunity, replied on Atharva's behalf in their native Telugu, expressing affection in words Atharva couldn't understand, but Raghu certainly did.

Atharva's panic soared as Raghu proudly announced that he had declared love on his behalf.

Feeling trapped and uncertain, Atharva grappled with the whirlwind of emotions coursing through him.

Yet, Gayathri's response, complete with a heart emoji and a landline number, left him both intrigued and apprehensive.

The clock ticked towards 8:30 p.m., the appointed time for the phone call.

Atharva's nerves were on edge as he debated the risks of dialling the number. What if it was a prank? What if he was being set up?

Summoning all his courage, Atharva dialled the number, heart pounding in his chest.

As the line connected, he was met with Gayathri's warm voice on the other end, sending a jolt of relief and excitement coursing through him.

Though their conversation was brief, the connection they shared felt undeniable, leaving Atharva with a newfound sense of hope and anticipation for what lay ahead.

As Atharva hung up the phone, a smile crept onto his face, mingled with a hint of nervousness.

Though he hadn't uttered the words "I love you" himself, the path before him seemed clearer now, guided by the unexpected twists and turns of fate and the quiet courage found within. And as he glanced at Raghu, he couldn't help but feel grateful for the friend who had unwittingly sparked the beginning of something extraordinary.

♥

Chapter Three

In the bustling corridors of their school, Atharva and Gayathri revelled in the sanctuary of their love, feeling as if the world around them faded into insignificance.

Their daily ritual of calling each other at 8:30 p.m. became sacrosanct, a lifeline that tethered them together despite the miles that separated them.

Yet, unbeknownst to them, their love story had woven its way into unexpected places.

Atharva's sister, Mithra, used to call Shruthi's home, and Shruthi's mother would often pick up the phone.

Mithra would chat briefly with Shruthi's mother, saying she was a friend.

Once Shruthi's mother handed the phone to Shruthi, Atharva would eagerly snatch the phone and talk with Shruthi for hours.

Meanwhile, Atharva made it a habit to walk past Gayathri's house every evening at 9:30, where she would stand by the window, her presence a silent affirmation of their connection.

As their bond deepened, Atharva couldn't shake the nagging doubts that clouded his mind.

Why did Gayathri entertain the attention of another boy (Mamul) while he was away? Was it mere infatuation, or did she truly love him? Despite his insecurities, he lacked the courage to confront the tumultuous thoughts swirling within him.

However, fate had a way of unravelling secrets, and soon, the shadow of scrutiny cast itself upon their love.

Gayathri's mother, a mathematics teacher at their school, caught wind of the whispers surrounding her daughter's affections. With a mixture of apprehension and determination, she summoned Atharva, sending a tremor of fear coursing through his veins.

Terrified of losing everything he held dear, Atharva found himself standing at the edge of the school swimming pool, grappling with the overwhelming weight of uncertainty.

But with trembling resolve, he took hesitant steps towards Gayathri's mother, steeling himself for the confrontation that awaited.

♥

As they exchanged pleasantries, Atharva's heart pounded in his chest, his mind racing with the fear of rejection.

Yet, in the midst of their conversation, Shruthi's mother didn't ask him the question he had been dreading and expecting, leaving Atharva momentarily surprised and relieved, dispelling the darkness of doubt that had clouded Atharva's mind.

Rushing to Gayathri, Atharva spilled his heart, recounting the encounter with her mother and the newfound clarity it had bestowed upon him.

In that moment, amidst the chaos and uncertainty, their love found strength in vulnerability, blossoming anew with each word shared between them.

On a calm day, Atharva asked Shruthi about Mamul. Despite the serene setting, he couldn't get a proper eye-to-eye response from her.

She simply looked away and said, "Forget the incident," leaving Atharva with more questions than answers.

♥

As the school bus wound its way through the picturesque countryside, Gayathri and Atharva could hardly contain their excitement.

They were on a school trip to Badami, a place steeped in history and mystery.

The anticipation bubbled within them as they imagined the adventures that awaited amidst the ancient world.

Their first stop was the awe-inspiring rock-cut sculptures, where history whispered in every carving.

Holding each other close, they wandered through the labyrinthine chambers, marvelling at the intricate sculptures and ancient inscriptions.

Amidst the ancient echoes, their love blossomed like a lotus in bloom.

"In Badami's embrace, where crimson sculptures rise,
Gayathri and Atharva found love's endless skies.
Amongst the ancient art, where stories unfold,
Their love story blossomed, radiant and bold.

Hand in hand, they wandered through time,
In the echoes of history, their hearts would chime.
Amidst the carvings of gods and kings,
Their love soared on whispered wings.

Beneath Badami's azure skies,
They found a love that never dies.
In the shadows of the rock-cut art,
They danced together like ocean waves.

Gayathri, with eyes like starlit nights,
Atharva, with a heart as bold as the sun's light.
In Badami's enchantment, they found their fate.
Bound by love, they would never hesitate.

Through the labyrinth of ancient streets,
They walked hand in hand, their love complete.
In the timeless beauty of Badami's embrace,
Gayathri and Atharva found their sacred place.

In Badami's heart, where legends reside,
Their love story would forever endure.
For in each other's arms, they found their home.

♥

Chapter Four

Air Marshal Atharva! Air Marshal Atharva!

Atharva stirred from his slumber, jolted awake by the urgent summons that echoed through his quarters.

Air Marshal Atharva!" the voice called out, shattering the silence of the room. With a sense of urgency, he demanded to know who had entered without permission, his authority palpable even in the dim light of dawn.

Lieutenant Sankalp, standing at attention, offered his apologies for the intrusion, explaining that urgent matters demanded immediate attention.

Atharva's brows furrowed in annoyance as he questioned why technology hadn't been utilised to convey the message.

"We don't have access to technology, sir," Sankalp replied, his voice tinged with a sense of apprehension.

As Atharva absorbed the gravity of the situation, his mind raced to comprehend the implications of what he was about to hear.

A world plunged into chaos by the sudden shutdown of the internet.

Communication was severed, satellites rendered useless, and the very fabric of society unravelled without the digital lifeline that had become so ingrained in everyday life.

With a mixture of disbelief and concern, Atharva listened as Sankalp explained the dire consequences of the internet blackout.

Without access to online services, people struggled to navigate even the simplest tasks of daily life.

From banking to social interaction, the reliance on technology had left society vulnerable and unprepared for such a catastrophic event.

As the weight of the situation settled upon him, Atharva couldn't help but marvel at the irony of humanity's dependence on technology.

In a world where smartphones had become extensions of the self, the sudden loss of connectivity had left people adrift, grappling with the most basic of tasks without the aid of digital assistance.

Despite the severity of the crisis, a small smile tugged at the corners of Atharva's lips as he rose from his chair.

In a world where intelligence was often equated with technological prowess, he couldn't help but find a hint of amusement in the realisation that, perhaps, humanity had grown a bit too reliant on its gadgets over the years.

As Atharva made his way towards the battalion headquarters, a sense of purpose drove him forward.

He was determined to take command and address the internet disruption that threatened to paralyse their operations.

But as he ascended the stairs, a sudden gunshot shattered the tranquillity of the Air Force base.

The sharp sound echoed through the air, followed by frantic shouts from his fellow officers.

Atharva's heart skipped a beat as he felt a searing pain tear through his chest.

The world seemed to spin as he struggled to catch his breath, his uniform stained crimson with blood.

Despite the chaos around him, Atharva's thoughts drifted to Gayathri Shruthi, his anchor in the storm.

Through the haze of pain and confusion, memories of their love story flickered like distant stars in the night sky.

As he lay there, fighting to stay conscious, Atharva heard the urgent voices of his comrades urging him towards the Air Force hospital.

The truth emerged amidst the chaos: the gunshot had come from a misfire during a training exercise, not an external attack.

With every laboured breath, Atharva reassured his comrades that the nation was safe and that the battalion was not in danger.

Despite the excruciating pain radiating from his chest, he clung to the memories of his love for Gayathri, finding solace in the beauty of their shared moments.

As medical personnel rushed to his aid, Atharva's thoughts lingered on the love that had sustained him through the darkest of times.

♥

Chapter Five

As the bus rumbled through the night, Atharva and Shruthi found themselves surrounded by a sea of sleepy passengers.

The weariness of the day's adventures weighed heavily on everyone's eyelids, yet amidst the darkness, a spark of connection ignited between them.

Seated at the front, Shruthi's silhouette was barely discernible in the dim light of the bus.

Atharva, unable to resist the magnetic pull of her presence, stealthily made his way towards her, clutching his precious MP4 player filled with Gayathri's favourite songs.

With a soft smile, he settled into the seat beside her, the anticipation of their shared moment palpable in the air.

In the quiet of the night, their hands found each other, fingers intertwining in a silent promise of companionship.

Atharva's gaze lingered on Shruthi's mesmerising eyes, losing himself in their depths as if nothing else existed in the world.

But then, a passing car illuminated the interior of the bus, casting a soft glow upon Shruthi's delicate features.

In that fleeting moment, Atharva's eyes fell upon her lips, delicate and inviting in the gentle light.

It was a sight he had never truly seen before, and for a moment, he was captivated by their beauty.

With a shy smile, Atharva presented the earphones to Shruthi, his heart pounding with anticipation.

As the music began to play, a blush crept onto Shruthi's cheeks, her hand tightening around his in a silent gesture of gratitude and affection.

But just as the melody of their favourite song filled the air, disaster struck.

The MP4 player, faithful companion to their journey, betrayed them with a flicker of its dying battery.

Atharva's heart sank as he attempted to revive it, his efforts proving futile in the face of its demise.

Yet, in that moment of disappointment, Shruthi's gentle voice whispered words of reassurance, her warm breath caressing his ear.

With a tender gesture, she drew closer, her lips brushing against his in a fleeting kiss that left Atharva breathless.

As the bus rumbled on into the night, Atharva couldn't shake the blush from his cheeks nor the warmth that lingered on his lips.

In the darkness of the bus, amidst the tired sighs of fellow travellers, a new chapter of their love story had begun, illuminated by the gentle glow of their shared connection.

The joy of the journey came to an abrupt halt as the destination loomed ahead.

Stepping off the bus into the drizzling night, Atharva scanned the crowd of parents and students, his heart racing with anticipation.

Amidst the darkness, he caught sight of a girl holding a green umbrella, her gaze locking with his before she turned away and disappeared into the night.

Without hesitation, Atharva followed, keeping a cautious distance as they traversed the midnight streets.

♥

Chapter Six

The beckoning call of the green umbrella compelled him forward, each step bringing him closer to his elusive companion.

But just as they neared their destination, she vanished into the darkness, leaving Atharva to wonder if she had ever been there at all.

The next day dawned with unexpected consequences. Atharva found himself singled out during the school's mass drill, forced to run laps as punishment for his absence during the previous mass drill.

Despite his efforts to keep his nighttime escapade a secret, a stern physical trainer confronted him, revealing that he knew the truth of what had happened last night.

As Atharva endured the humiliation of running laps on the soggy ground, he couldn't shake the feeling of being betrayed.

When he returned to the classroom, he was met with a barrage of questions and accusations from the teachers, their words cutting deep as they questioned his dedication to his studies.

Feeling the weight of their judgement, Atharva refused to back down; his pride was wounded, but his resolve was unbroken.

Though he knew the road ahead would be fraught with challenges, he remained determined to persevere, refusing to let anyone dictate his path in life.

But deep down, he couldn't shake the suspicion that Shruthi's mother had orchestrated his humiliation, using external pressures to force him into submission.

Despite the turmoil swirling around him, Atharva vowed to stay true to himself, even if it meant facing the consequences of his feelings for Shruthi head-on.

♥

Chapter Seven

At 8 p.m., the familiar ringtone echoed through Atharva's room, signalling the start of their nightly ritual.

But this time, it wasn't Atharva dialling Shruthi's number—it was a call coming from her end.

A sense of unease settled over him, sensing that something was amiss.

The line fell silent for what felt like an eternity, the tension thickening with each passing second.

Then, in a hushed voice barely audible over the line, Shruthi uttered words that sent shockwaves through Atharva's being.

"Can you please stop calling me every day and talking to me," she murmured, her words carrying a weight that Atharva struggled to comprehend. Was she asking him to stop talking to her altogether, or was it a plea to cease his expressions of love?

Confusion clouded Atharva's mind as he grappled with the sudden turn of events.

Their love had only just begun to blossom, and now it seemed to hang in the balance, teetering on the edge of uncertainty.

Atharva felt as though a bolt of lightning had struck him, leaving him reeling in its wake.

Clutching the phone tightly, Atharva's heart pounded with anticipation, his breaths shallow as he awaited her response.

But all he could hear was the sound of soft weeping, tearing at his soul with each sob.

Unable to bear the sight of her tears, Atharva pleaded for an explanation, his voice trembling with emotion.

Yet, before he could make sense of her words, Shruthi's voice cut through the silence one last time: a whispered plea to refrain from asking further questions.

With a heavy heart, she ended the call, leaving Atharva to grapple with the whirlwind of emotions that threatened to consume him.

Alone in the darkness, he couldn't shake the feeling of uncertainty that now clouded their once-bright future together.

The night had been a restless blur for Atharva.

Sleep had eluded him; his mind was consumed by a whirlwind of confusion and unanswered questions.

As dawn broke, he awoke with a start, his thoughts still tangled in the events of the previous night.

With a sense of urgency coursing through his veins, Atharva rose early, his mind a blank canvas desperate for answers.

"What happened? I need to get to school," he exclaimed, his voice raw with emotion, startling everyone at home with his sudden outburst.

Snatching up his bag, he felt a weightlessness settle over him; an unsettling discomfort gnawed at his insides.

Every interaction felt strained; every moment tinged with an unspoken tension as he hurried towards the familiar halls of his school.

His heart raced as he scanned the crowded corridors, searching for a glimpse of her familiar figure.

With each passing moment, his desperation grew; his breaths came in short, ragged gasps as he darted from one corner to the next.

Then, amidst the throng of students, he spotted her—standing on the balcony of the first floor, laughter dancing on her lips as she conversed with a friend. But as Atharva approached, his hopes were dashed in an instant.

She turned away, her gaze fixed on the ground as she hurried past him, leaving him to grapple with the emptiness that threatened to consume him.

It felt as though he had been cast out from the heights of the first floor to the cold, unforgiving ground below.

With a heavy heart, Atharva made his way to the school assembly, his eyes scanning the crowd for a sign of her presence.

But she remained resolutely distant, her eyes squeezed shut as if unwilling to meet his gaze.

As the morning assembly began, Atharva's thoughts were consumed by the image of her closed eyes, a silent plea echoing in his heart for just a single glance in his direction.

But she remained steadfast in her refusal, leaving him to navigate the day with a heavy heart and a mind consumed by thoughts of her.

Each passing minute felt like an eternity; each moment stretched on as he waited for the chance to bridge the growing chasm between them.

His mind buzzed with unresolved thoughts, his usual focus slipping through his fingers like grains of sand.

Despite his best efforts, he found it difficult to concentrate on the lessons; his attention wandered as he struggled to make sense of the turmoil within.

In social science class, the teacher recounted the tale of the collapse of the Indus Valley civilisation, painting a vivid picture of a once-great empire brought to its knees by internal strife and external pressures.

Atharva found himself drawn to the story of war and upheaval, his mind wandering into the depths of history as he pondered the reasons behind the civilisation's downfall.

As the teacher emphasised the importance of accepting change in order to survive, a profound realisation dawned on Atharva.

Acceptance of the shifting currents of life was not just a lesson from the past; it was a message for the present moment.

Like the ancient peoples of the Indus Valley, they too faced a changing landscape, one where love and relationships had shifted and evolved.

With a heavy heart, Atharva acknowledged the truth of his situation. Shruthi had changed, and so had their love.

But clinging to the past would only lead to further pain and isolation.

If he wanted to move forward, he needed to embrace the changes around him, no matter how difficult or painful they may be.

In that moment of clarity, Atharva made a silent vow to himself. He would not let the turbulence of life break him.

Instead, he would adapt, he would evolve, and he would survive.

For acceptance of change was not just a lesson — it was the key to unlocking a brighter, more resilient future.

The urge to unleash his pent-up sorrow and frustration simmered within him, begging for release.

But where could he direct this overwhelming energy? Who could bear the burden of his turmoil?

As the bell rang, signalling the end of class, a surge of students flooded towards the school grounds, eager to revel in the freedom of play. Atharva found himself swept up in the rush, his feet carrying him towards a circle of volleyball players.

Joining the game with newfound vigour, Atharva threw himself into the fray.

His movements became fluid, his actions driven by an intensity he hadn't known he possessed. With each jump, each spike, he channelled his emotions into the game, pushing himself to his limits.

As the match intensified, so did the aggression of both teams.

The air crackled with tension, each player pushing themselves to the brink in pursuit of victory.

But as the bell rang once more, signalling the end of the game, a palpable sense of camaraderie replaced the earlier hostility.

No winner was declared; no loser conceded defeat.

Yet, amidst the shared exhaustion and exhilaration, a profound sense of satisfaction lingered on the field.

Like heroes after battle, the players clasped hands and made their way back to the classroom. Atharva's mind was finally clear and his spirit was uplifted.

Atharva trudged towards the school's exit, his expression heavy with unanswered questions.

"Stop calling me every day and just don't talk to me," she had said, her words still echoing in his mind.

As he walked, he noticed a familiar bag hurrying past him in a passing breeze.

It was hers.

She swept through the school gates, and in that moment, she turned and flashed a smile.

♥

Atharva was speechless, unsure of how to react to her sudden change in demeanour.

He found himself compelled to follow her, seeking the answers he so desperately sought.

A sudden thunderstorm descended upon the city, transforming the once-sunny skies into a tumultuous sea of clouds.

Atharva's heart pounded in his chest, momentarily forgetting his sorrows and disappointments.

She halted in the middle of the road and hailed an auto, seemingly unperturbed by the impending rain.

Atharva tried to convince himself that she was merely seeking shelter from the downpour, but as the raindrops began to fall, he found himself standing mesmerised, letting the cool drops wash over him.

Memories flooded his mind—the touch of her lips, the anticipation of seeing her, the hours spent waiting just for a glimpse of her.

As thunder rumbled in the distance, Atharva felt a sense of connection, as if the storm mirrored the turmoil within him.

But when he finally laid eyes on her, standing there in the rain, he felt a sense of renewal wash over him.

Like the parched earth drinking in the rain, he too felt refreshed, as if her presence had brought solace to his troubled soul.

♥

Atharva stood beneath the darkening sky, raindrops beginning to pelt down around him. Instead of seeking shelter, he found himself drawn to the storm, as if the falling rain held the answers to the questions that plagued his mind.

He tilted his head back, watching the clouds shift and morph with each passing moment; a silent conversation unfolding above him.

Amidst the rhythmic pattern of rain, Atharva's ears caught the ethereal strains of a veena drifting from a nearby window.

The haunting melody seemed to underscore the silence that enveloped him; a silence that echoed with the weight of unspoken words and unanswered emotions.

In the midst of the tumultuous storm, Atharva found himself yearning not for her words, but for her silence—for the unspoken truths that lingered between them.

His longing for her voice, her presence, was suddenly interrupted by the unexpected arrival of an auto; its unfamiliar honk cutting through the din of the rain.

Startled, Atharva turned to see Shruthi, the girl who had left him just minutes before.

Without a word, she reached out and grasped his hand, pulling him into the shelter of the rain-drenched auto.

As they sat together in the intimate space, Shurthi nestled against his shoulder, her breathing slow and steady.

In that moment of quiet communion, Atharva felt a sense of peace settle over him, as if the final ache of longing had been soothed by her mere presence.

No words were exchanged between them, no explanations offered—and yet, in the silence, Atharva found a profound understanding.

As they continued on their journey through the storm-lashed streets, Atharva let go of the questions that had plagued him all day, allowing himself to simply be present in the moment.

In the gentle embrace of the rain and the whispering breeze, he found solace, knowing that in the touch of his love, all was right with the world.

In that fleeting moment of connection, Atharva understood that no matter what trials they faced, as long as they faced them together, they would emerge unscathed, their love a beacon of light in the darkness.

As the auto came to a stop, Shurthi released her grip on Atharva's hand, her movements deliberate and resolute.

Stepping out into the rain-soaked street, she put distance between them, her voice carrying through the downpour.

"Forget me," she implored, her words heavy with emotion. "It's for the best."

Don't ask me why; I have no answers." But Atharva refused to look away, his gaze searching her eyes for any hint of the truth.

He sensed she was holding something back, a weighty secret hidden beneath the surface.

Desperate for understanding, Atharva reached out to her once more, but Shurthi shook her head, her resolve unwavering.

With one final glance, she disappeared into the mist of rain, leaving Atharva alone with his thoughts.

Suddenly, a deafening clap of thunder shattered the air, reverberating through Atharva's chest like a physical blow.

It was as if the storm itself mirrored the turmoil in his heart, the pain of rejection cutting deep despite the absence of a clear reason.

As the rain continued to fall, Atharva stood alone in the empty street, grappling with the ache of loss and the unanswered questions that echoed in his mind.

As Atharva lay on the operating table, the doctor said, "Let's remove the bullet, and everything will be fine."

"Surrounded by the sterile environment of the operation theatre, he felt a strange sensation gripping his chest.

It was as if someone was reaching into his heart, probing the depths and attempting to extract something hidden within.

The pain, though dulled by anaesthesia, still pulsed through him, a reminder of the bullets that had pierced his body mere hours before.

In the hazy realm between consciousness and unconsciousness, Atharva could hear the distant rumble of thunder echoing through the hospital walls.

It was a sound that seemed to reverberate within him, matching the rhythm of his own heartbeat.

But unlike the booming thunder, Atharva remained still, unable to react to the pain that gnawed at his insides.

As Atharva lay on the operating table, his senses dulled by anaesthesia but still aware of the faint sounds and sensations around him, his mind drifted back to the pain when Shurthi had walked away from him without explanation.

It was a memory etched into his consciousness with painful clarity; each detail was vivid and raw.

He recalled the way her voice had trembled as she uttered those final words, her eyes betraying a sadness he couldn't quite comprehend.

Why had she left? What had he done wrong? The lack of closure gnawed at him, leaving him feeling adrift in a sea of uncertainty.

And now, as he lay on the brink of unconsciousness in the sterile confines of the operation theatre, the physical pain of the bullets lodged within him served as a stark reminder of the emotional turmoil he had endured.

It was a pain that seemed to seep into every fibre of his being, relentless and unforgiving.

In that moment, the parallels between the two forms of agony became all too clear to Atharva.

Just as the bullets tore through his flesh, leaving behind a trail of destruction, so too had Shurthi's departure ripped through his heart, leaving behind a gaping wound that refused to heal.

Both pains were inexplicable, defying logic and reason.

And yet, they shared a common thread of helplessness and confusion that bound them together.

Atharva couldn't shake the feeling that he was being consumed by forces beyond his control, swept away by the relentless tide of fate.

As Atharva walked towards the quiet solitude of the evening, he felt a sense of calm wash over him. But suddenly, as he entered the home, the tranquillity was shattered by the ringing of his phone.

It was Shurthi, calling in tears, her voice heavy with sorrow.

"You won't be a part of this school anymore," she sobbed. "My mother is doing everything she can to get you removed from here. She's afraid we'll keep loving each other."

A wave of confusion and frustration washed over Atharva as he listened to her words.

He couldn't understand why their relationship was being torn apart.

Earlier that day, he had sat down and tried to make sense of it all.

He was seen as weak, unable to impress others with his academic achievements.

And to make matters worse, he was just a young boy, not yet considered old enough to be in love, especially with the daughter of a teacher from their own school.

Society would never accept it.

Despite his efforts to rationalise the situation, Atharva felt completely helpless.

He had no one to confide in, no one to share his thoughts and fears with.

Atharva stood before the radio, his trembling hand pressing play on the song 'Tu Mile, Dil Khile,' a song he had recorded with immense difficulty.

Leaning heavily on the stand, he listened to the haunting melody, his ears pressed close to the speaker.

Tears streamed down his face as he felt the weight of his sorrow bearing down on him.

In a desperate attempt to drown out the pain, he repeatedly pressed the reverse button, each repetition of the song's lyrics— 'Tu Mile, Dil Khile, Aur Jeene Ko Kya Chahiye, Na Ho Tu Udaas, Tere Paas Paas, Main Rahoonga Zindagi Bhar'—echoing the tragedy that had befallen his life.

He longed to scream, to release the overwhelming sadness that threatened to consume him entirely.

But instead, he found solace in the melancholic melody, allowing it to envelop him in its bittersweet embrace.

♥

Shruthi waited in the dim glow of the room, watching as the lights flickered and eventually faded, signalling the silence that enveloped her home.

As the minutes passed and the house fell into a slumbering stillness, she felt the weight of her emotions begin to crush her.

Tears streamed down her cheeks; her sobs muffled by the pillow pressed against her face, desperate to conceal the sound of her anguish.

In the darkness, she wrestled with her inner turmoil, her breaths coming in ragged gasps as she struggled to contain the storm raging within her.

Why couldn't things unfold as she had hoped and dreamed? Why did she yearn for him so deeply, only to be met with disappointment and heartache?

The pain of her unfulfilled desires gnawed at her soul, leaving her feeling lost and alone in the silence of the night.

♥

Chapter Eight

As Atharva gradually stirred from his slumber in the hospital bed, he felt a twinge of discomfort near his chest.

With a sigh, he opened his eyes and greeted the people around him, expressing his gratitude for their efforts in saving him from the unexpected bullet wound.

Despite the pain, he managed a small smile, his eyes conveying a silent plea to the officers present to handle the situation with care, assuming that the officer who had fired the shot had no malicious intent.

As Atharva tried to adjust to his surroundings, another officer approached him with a solemn expression.

"The decorated chief of our nation, the president, wishes to speak with you," the officer informed him.

Atharva nodded, his curiosity piqued. "Yes, please go ahead," he replied, bracing himself for the conversation that was about to unfold.

President: "Jai Hind! How are you feeling now? Is everything alright? Do you want anything from the nation?"

Atharva: (struggling with the pain in his chest) "Jai Hind! I am doing well, sir. Thank you for your concern. It's an honour to serve the nation."

President: (in a commanding tone) "I believe you are aware of the situation happening in the country. The nation is working hard to fix the problem of internet outrage. But we know you are one of the finest officers the nation has seen. We want you to rest, Atharva."

Atharva: "Thank you, sir. But I will recover soon and be a part of resolving the crisis."

President: "Jai Hind, Atharva."

Atharva: "Jai Hind, sir."

He felt a swell of pride as the nation rallied around him, offering well wishes and acknowledging his contributions to the country.

♥

Chapter Nine

As Atharva's daughter, Sana, rushed towards him, her innocent eyes widened in concern as she noticed the bandage covering her father's chest. "Daddy, why is it covered? You know this is where I sleep every day."

How will I sleep comfortably now?" she questioned, her voice tinged with worry.

A soft, gentle smile spread across Atharva's face as he looked upon the love that radiated from his daughter.

"That place will always be yours, Sana. You can still sleep there," he reassured her, his voice filled with tenderness.

But Sana, being very young and unable to fully comprehend the gravity of the situation, insisted, "You promised we would go out to play, Daddy!" Her tears threatened to spill over as she clung to the promise her father had made.

Despite the protests of those around him, Atharva could not bear to see his daughter upset.

"Yes, we will go out," he promised, longing to bring a smile back to her face.

As the room emptied, father and daughter were left alone, and Sana leaped into her father's arms.

Though Atharva winced at the pain in his chest, he resisted the urge to pull away, holding his daughter close.

"Daddy, for the next few days, can you carry me on your shoulders?" Sana asked eagerly, her eyes shining with excitement.

Atharva couldn't help but chuckle at her enthusiasm. "Of course, princess," he replied, his heart swelling with love for his daughter.

As he began to dress her, Sana's excitement turned to disappointment. "But I want to wear traditional clothes!" she exclaimed, her bottom lip quivering.

"Alright, let's go like this," he agreed, seeing the spark of joy return to her eyes.

But when Sana noticed her father's tired expression, she threw herself dramatically against the wall, pretending to cry.

Atharva couldn't help but smile at her antics, knowing that nothing was more important to him than his daughter's happiness.

Come now, my princess, he murmured softly, his voice a soothing balm. With tender hands, he reached for her, ready to lift her from the torment of her self-imposed exile—an aching silence carved deep within her chest, still raw from the surgery.

Atharva made the decision to take his daughter, Sana, to the temple. As they walked together, "I won't disappoint you," he assured her, determined to fulfil her wishes.

With a resounding "Okay, father!" Sana agreed eagerly, her voice echoing through the corridors of the temple.

As they entered, her eyes lit up at the sight of the stone-carved elephant, momentarily forgetting her earlier anger.

"Can we go see the elephant first?" she pleaded, her excitement bubbling over.

Atharva smiled and lifted her onto the elephant-shaped stone, watching as she joyfully swung her legs back and forth.

Her excitement only grew as they approached the illuminated Kalayani, her eyes wide with wonder at the flickering oil lamps.

"Let's go there now!" she exclaimed, settling herself next to a few of the lamps, her curiosity piqued as she observed their warm glow.

Bending down to examine the lamps more closely, Sana wrinkled her nose at the scent before eagerly studying their positions.

"Daddy, look! The wind is playing with the flames! Come see the colours," she called out, her enthusiasm infectious.

Her pupils glistened with such beauty; it was as if he was witnessing the most exquisite sight in the world.

Her innocent confusion only added to the charm of her face.

Lost in the moment, he noticed Sana beginning to yawn and stretch her hand lazily towards him.

Understanding her silent request, Atharva gently lifted her onto his shoulders and resumed their journey towards the temple, feeling a pain in his chest.

Once inside, Sana's attention was drawn to the temple bell, which she eagerly reached out to touch, citing Atharva to lift even more to touch the bell of the temple, her laughter ringing through the sacred space as she struck it with all her might.

Atharva watched with a sense of awe, realising the depth of his love and care for his daughter.

As he gazed upon her, he couldn't help but reflect on the profound truth he had discovered: "A man's true care and love take rebirth once he becomes a father."

Finally, Sana closed her eyes and clasped her hands in prayer, her face a mixture of confusion and reverence as she sought the presence of the divine.

Sana dashed towards the prasada distribution area, completely forgetting everything else as she exclaimed, "Daddy, this will be yummy! Follow me!"

However, her long skirt caused her to trip and fall. At that moment, Atharva felt a rush of emotion and panic as he swiftly scooped her up into his arms, reassuring her with a gentle "Sana,"

Refusing to be deterred, Sana declared herself to be a "superwoman," quickly straightening her dress before confidently striding towards the counter.

With determination, she collected the prasada on her own, carefully testing its temperature with her tiny finger. "Daddy, this is so yummy!"

"Why don't we cook food like this at home?" she asked, reaching out to take a bite before insisting that Atharva eat some as well, reserving the rest for her dinner.

As Sana observed the cooking vessels and the bustling kitchen nearby, her curiosity grew.

She bounded down the stairs, clumsily wiping her hands on her clothes before standing proudly with her hands on her hips, observing the cooking process with keen interest.

Sana dashed across the temple courtyard, her vibrant yellow traditional attire catching Atharva's attention as he sat and observed her with fondness.

The sun had begun its descent, casting golden rays that danced upon Sana's form, and Atharva couldn't help but marvel at the sight.

Suddenly, Sana turned back and sprinted towards Atharva, throwing her arms around him in a tight embrace.

Her expression was a mixture of confusion and joy as she nestled against him.

Atharva glanced towards a group of devotees approaching from the opposite direction, realising that Sana had been frightened to run between them and had sought refuge with him instead.

As Sana stretched out her hand towards Atharva's watch, she carefully removed it and attempted to wear it herself.

With a playful twinkle in her eye, she angled the watch face towards the sunlight, creating mesmerising reflections on the temple walls.

Delighted with her discovery, she giggled with excitement.

However, her joy was short-lived as she noticed a red mark on Atharva's shirt. Concerned, she pointed it out, exclaiming, "Daddy, look! There's blood!" Her hand flew to her mouth in shock, her eyes wide with worry.

"You're clumsy, Daddy. You're not as hygienic as me," she chided before bounding off towards a group of children playing nearby, eager to show off her watch tricks.

Atharva watched her go with a mixture of amusement and pride, his gaze lingering on the fading sunlight, obscured by the temple's towering gopuram.

As the melodic notes of the traditional song filled the air, all the children clad in vibrant traditional attire were ushered to sit behind the lead singer.

Sana, among them, sat in the row, her face a mask of indifference and amusement.

As the group of children began to sing along with the main singer, Sana tentatively tried to mimic the singer's gestures, tapping her hand to the rhythm.

Atharva, observing Sana, noticed a rare stability in her expression, a departure from her usual demeanour.

Suddenly, their eyes met, and Sana arched an eyebrow in silent acknowledgement of Atharva's presence among the spectators.

The captivating voice of the lead singer stirred memories within Atharva, transporting him back to an evening spent at the temple, listening to Shruthi's enchanting performance.

Chapter Ten

Atharva stood in the middle of the corridor, his heart heavy with the weight of uncertainty.

Gripping Shruthi's hand tightly, he pleaded, "I deserve to know the truth. Please, don't leave me in the dark."

Shruthi's eyes glistened with unshed tears as she whispered, "Can you let go of my hand, please?" But Atharva refused to release his grip, his determination unwavering.

Finally, with a trembling voice, Shruthi revealed the painful truth. "Last week, my father had a mild heart attack."

It happened after my mother found out about us and blamed me for the stress leading up to his surgery."

Her words hung heavy in the air, each syllable laden with sorrow. Atharva felt his own heartbreak as he listened to her explanation. Her tears flowed freely, her lips parched and trembling with emotion.

"Would you be okay if your daughter caused you the same pain?" she asked, her voice barely above a whisper.

Atharva remained silent, unable to find the words to respond.

Shruthi continued, her voice quivering with emotion.

"My mother threatened to blacklist you from all schools if our relationship continued.

And besides, we come from different communities. My family is very orthodox. We simply can't be together."

Atharva felt a sense of helplessness wash over him. He wanted to fight for their love, to defy the odds stacked against them.

But at that moment, he felt ill-equipped to do so.

He lacked the maturity and confidence to stand up to Shruthi's family and societal expectations.

"I won't leave you," Atharva declared, his voice tinged with desperation.

In a bold move, he reached for Shruthi's bag, took her wallet, and retrieved a passport-sized photo of her.

Tucking it into his pocket, he vowed silently to keep her close, no matter what obstacles they faced.

As he began to walk away, Atharva felt the eyes of the corridor upon them, witnesses to the raw emotion and undying love that bound him to Shruthi.

Though he moved backwards, his gaze remained fixed on her, silently promising that their love would endure, no matter the distance or challenges ahead.

The final exam season descended upon the school, casting a palpable aura of tension and anticipation.

Atharva, like many of his peers, found himself engulfed in a sea of uncertainty.

Lost in a whirlwind of academic struggles, he felt utterly adrift, unsure of where to begin or how to navigate the daunting task ahead.

As the days dwindled down to the eve of the final exam, Atharva's anxiety reached a fever pitch.

His mind raced with thoughts of inadequacy and failure; his confidence waning with each passing moment.

He knew that he had not been diligent enough in his studies, but the enormity of the impending exam left him paralysed with fear.

♥

Then, on the eve of the final exam, Atharva received an unexpected summons to the principal's office.

Confused and apprehensive, he made his way to the imposing doorway, his heart pounding in his chest.

Sitting across from the principal, Atharva braced himself for what he assumed would be a routine administrative matter.

The principal laid out his exam papers from the past week, revealing a stark truth that Atharva had been dreading: he had failed in all subjects.

The weight of his academic shortcomings bore down on him, crushing his spirit with each passing moment.

In a voice laced with concern and disappointment, the principal broached the subject of Atharva's academic performance.

She hinted at the possibility that he might be the reason for the school's potential decline in academic standings, suggesting that his failure could tarnish the school's reputation.

Offering him a lifeline amidst the storm of his despair, the principal presented Atharva with a choice:

She would manipulate his marks to ensure a passing grade, but in exchange, he would have to leave the school.

The prospect of starting anew in a different environment beckoned him, offering a glimmer of hope amidst the darkness of his current predicament.

Lost in a whirlwind of conflicting emotions, Atharva stepped outside the principal's office, his mind a tumultuous storm of doubts and fears.

How would he face his family with this devastating news? And what of Shruthi, the love of his life? Would she understand the gravity of his situation, or would she be consumed by disappointment and disillusionment?

As he grappled with these questions, Atharva felt a sense of profound isolation wash over him.

In the midst of his turmoil, he found himself standing at a crossroads, his future hanging in the balance.

With a heavy heart and a trembling voice, he made a decision that would alter the course of his life forever.

Returning to the principal's office, Atharva spoke with a quiet resolve, his voice ringing out with a newfound clarity.

"Please give me my transfer certificate," he said, his words heavy with resignation. "I will leave the school."

Though his heart ached with sorrow and regret, Atharva knew that sometimes, the hardest decisions were the ones that led to a brighter tomorrow.

As he walked away from the familiar halls of his school, he carried with him a flicker of hope, knowing that every mistake held the potential for growth and redemption.

As he walked through the familiar corridors of his school, Atharva couldn't shake the feeling of impending finality that hung in the air.

Each step seemed to echo with the weight of uncertainty, reminding him that this might be the last time he would walk these halls in his school uniform.

Approaching his friends, Atharva gathered the courage to share his truth with them.

However, to his dismay, they laughed off the idea of him leaving the school.

It seemed they couldn't fathom the notion of their friend departing from their midst.

With a heavy heart, Atharva realised that this day would be filled with bittersweet farewells.

Every corner of the school held memories of laughter, friendship, and shared experiences.

It wasn't just Shruthi who haunted his thoughts; it was the entire school, each hallway and classroom imbued with a sense of nostalgia and finality.

Desperately clinging to the present moment, Atharva rushed to drink from the water fountain one last time, savouring the taste of familiarity.

He joined his friends for lunch, relishing the simple pleasure of sharing a meal together for the last time.

As he walked through the corridors, Atharva couldn't help but dwell on the uncertainty of the future.

Inside, Atharva felt like a hollow silence, a painful void he couldn't express.

Shruthi had given him dreams and faded behind the stage, leaving their memories scattered like whispers in the empty school corridors.

It felt as if a mother had abandoned her child in a bustling street, or as if a stream had suddenly ceased its flow.

"Our picture is unfinished," he thought, "and perhaps it will remain that way."

"Everything felt suspended, incomplete. And yet, he knew—only Shruthi could rekindle that feeling; only she could make it whole again."

He wished all that had happened was nothing but a fleeting nightmare.

"Don't go missing, just to see what would happen. I feel there's still a chapter left for us, a page waiting to be written," he whispered to himself. "My sunshine, don't leave me. My breath, don't stop breathing."

With a heavy heart and a sense of resignation, Atharva realised that sometimes life's journey took unexpected turns.

As he prepared to bid farewell to his school days, he knew that the road ahead would be filled with challenges and uncertainties.

But he also held onto the hope that amidst the turmoil, he would find the strength to carve out a new path for himself, one filled with possibility and promise.

As Atharva strolled along the school road for what he knew would be the final time, he observed the bustling activity around him.

Each person seemed engrossed in their own world, unaware of the tumult of emotions raging within him.

With each step, Atharva felt a pang of sorrow deep within his chest. As he reached the end of the road, a profound sense of finality washed over him.

It was here, at this symbolic endpoint, that he made a decision.

In a moment of quiet desperation, Atharva reached for the button of his shirt and deftly undid it.

With a heavy heart, he whispered, "You're not mine anymore."

As the button slipped from his fingers, it felt like a tangible release from the memories and dreams he had cherished.

With that simple gesture, Atharva let go of the past, allowing his dreams of Shruthi to fade into the distance.

Though the road ahead was uncertain, he knew that he had to leave behind the echoes of what could have been and embrace the journey that lay ahead.

♥

Chapter Eleven

"Daddy, Daddy, are you okay?" said Sana softly. Atharva noticed the concern etched on his daughter's face as she frantically pointed to the bloodstain on his shirt.

His heart clenched with a mixture of tenderness and sadness as he gazed at her innocent eyes, brimming with worry.

"It's alright, sweetheart," he reassured her, mustering a faint smile despite the ache in his chest. "Just a little discomfort, that's all."

Sana's brows furrowed in confusion, her eyes widening as she noticed the glistening tear that lingered at the corner of Atharva's eye.

"But why are you crying, Daddy? Does it hurt a lot?" she asked, her voice tinged with concern.

Atharva's breath caught in his throat, a wave of emotion crashing over him as he struggled to find the words to comfort his daughter.

"No, darling, it's not that," he replied, his voice barely above a whisper. "Sometimes, tears are just a way for our hearts to speak when words fail us."

As the last rays of sunlight disappeared behind the temple's towering gopuram, Atharva felt a sense of closure wash over him.

The darkness that had clouded his thoughts of Shruthi seemed to lift, replaced by a glimmer of acceptance and peace.

With Sana's gentle presence by his side, Atharva realised that while some chapters of his life had come to an end, new beginnings awaited on the horizon.

And as he watched the fading light of the day, "With each day's end comes the promise of a new dawn."

♥

Chapter Twelve

As Atharva made his way towards the temple, a profound realisation struck him like a bolt of lightning.

He couldn't shake the thought that what Shruthi's mother had done was indeed right.

She was not just a teacher; she was a mentor, a guide to countless students.

How deeply she must have felt the weight of her own actions.

Yes, it was his mistake, perhaps a mistake that ultimately led him to become the successful person he was today.

Turning towards the temple, Atharva offered up a silent prayer for forgiveness. "Forgive me," he whispered, "but grant me the opportunity to make a difference."

With resolve in his heart, he settled into the car and retrieved a piece of paper.

As his daughter Sana gazed out the window, lost in her own thoughts, Atharva dialled the number of an old friend, Veeru, who happened to be a cabinet minister in their home state.

"Marshal, how are you feeling?" Veeru's voice crackled over the line, concern evident in his tone.

Atharva assured him of his recovery and proceeded to outline a draft policy he had in mind.

♥

There was an issue of internet outrage across the nation, but this was different - something close to his heart.

Veeru readily agreed to implement the policy, promising to pass the order overnight.

Days passed, and Atharva received a message from Veeru urging him to check the news.

With a sense of anticipation, Atharva walked to the living room and turned on the television.

There, he saw Veeru seated amidst a group of teachers, holding a paper in his hand.

The teachers looked bewildered, unsure of what the minister was about to announce.

Veeru's voice resonated through the screen as he declared, "Today, we recognise the invaluable contributions of our teachers to society."

"Acharyaḥ pātram *vyākhyānaḥ "*

This translates to "A teacher is the vessel of knowledge and its explanation," emphasising the role of a teacher as the carrier and transmitter of wisdom.

They endure countless hours and years standing side by side, imparting knowledge to us.

In honour of their dedication and service, the government is pleased to announce a new policy."

He went on to explain that all teachers, regardless of their background or school affiliation, would be eligible for free knee-cap replacement surgeries at any hospital in the state.

The room erupted in applause, tears of gratitude shining in the eyes of the teachers.

Veeru continued addressing other pressing issues. Teachers continue to use chalk to write on the board, but they are facing eye issues as a result, such as eye treatments, and emphasising the government's commitment to providing free (without any clause) eye treatment from basic to surgery.

Atharva couldn't help but smile as he witnessed the joy and relief on the faces of those who had devoted their lives to teaching.

As the press inquired about the cost of such initiatives, Veeru confidently replied that the government would bear all expenses.

One teacher spoke up, expressing gratitude for addressing their real future problems.

Atharva watched, his heart swelling with pride and contentment, knowing that he had played a small part in bringing about positive change for those who dedicated their lives to shaping the future generation.

As he flips through the TV channels, he catches sight of a Dalai Lama speech.

It brings back memories of the first speech given to him on a train by a sassy monk and a blind guy after he left school, and he slowly goes to sleep.

♥

Chapter Thirteen

Atharva found himself inching towards the corner of the line, feeling utterly lacking in confidence as he tried to blend into the unfamiliar surroundings of the new school.

Tentatively, he extended his hand to greet the new faces around him, all the while absorbing the instructions being given for the selection process.

Standing in line, he listened attentively to the commands: "Hands at your back... Stand in line... Maintain height."

It felt as though he was passively accepting everything that was being directed at him, surrendering himself to the new environment.

Amidst the murmurs, he caught wind of something called NCC, the National Cadet Corps.

Puzzled, he wondered what it entailed. Someone mentioned that it involved activities like a march past and that it could mean skipping classes on Saturdays.

Feeling disconnected from sports and doubting his abilities, Atharva assumed he would be rejected in no time.

It seemed like another instance where he would face disappointment, adding to the rejection he had experienced in the past.

As the selection process progressed, an officer eventually directed him to a separate corner, mentally categorising him as part of the rejected group.

The announcement that attendance at NCC practice sessions was required every Saturday only added to Atharva's disinterest in life.

Nevertheless, resigned to the whims of fate, he thought, "Chalo... Nothing is going as I wish. Let life decide its course."

"It was as if destiny was steering him towards the fulfilment of his aspirations, albeit in unexpected ways."

♥

Then came the unexpected journey to his grandparents' place, a solo trip on the train.

Suddenly, Atharva found himself in the company of two individuals on the train: a blind man and a well-dressed man who exudes an air of sassiness, almost resembling a monk - a sassy monk.

Initially, Atharva had no intention of engaging in conversation with them.

However, as the journey progressed, Atharva couldn't help but notice the charismatic monk-like figure sitting beside him.

The man broke the silence by asking Atharva where he was headed. Atharva replied with a nod, indicating that he was travelling to the last stop of the train.

Curious, the sassy monk inquired about Atharva's studies.

Atharva hesitated at first, but then admitted that he was currently preparing for his board exams.

With a chuckle, the monk encouraged him to be happy and questioned why he seemed so down.

He eagerly steered the conversation toward a topic that sparked excitement in him; his eyes lighting up with enthusiasm.

Meanwhile, the blind man nearby attempted to subtly listen in on their discussion.

The sassy monk leaned in and shared some words of wisdom with the kid sitting next to him.

He explained that in life, people often think that once you accomplish something like finishing your board exams, everything is sorted.

But then comes another challenge, like the 12th board exams, and the cycle repeats itself.

Even after getting a degree, there are more expectations, like finding a job, getting married, and starting a family.

However, the monk emphasised that life is not a set path for everyone.

Each person's journey is unique, with its own surprises and discoveries.

He pointed out that the cycle of life repeats itself, from going to school to seeing your own children go through the same process.

But the monk didn't want the kid to feel overwhelmed by this cycle.

Instead, he encouraged the kid to find balance and not to stress too much about following society's expectations.

Life, he said, is meant to be enjoyed and embraced, even with its ups and downs.

The blind man chimed in, acknowledging the sassy monk's words. He agreed that understanding life can sometimes feel overwhelming.

However, he emphasised the importance of discipline and honesty, stating that they are invaluable skills.

He explained that it's not just about passing exams or following a predetermined path, but about carving out one's own journey.

The blind man encouraged Atharva to listen to his heart and ensure that his words and actions aligned with his true intentions. He emphasised the importance of staying true to oneself, as inner thoughts will always reveal the truth.

With a smile, the sassy monk added that luck is not the determining factor in life.

Instead, it's the decisions we make and the intentions behind them.

He reassured Atharva that life is beautiful when guided by the right decisions and intentions. You end up in bad luck only if you make wrong decisions.

Atharva found himself speechless yet captivated by the conversation, which lasted for three hours.

He couldn't help but wonder why moral topics weren't discussed in school. Despite this, he managed to grasp the key points of the discussion.

It struck him that this was the first time he had ever listened intently for such a long duration.

He silently applauded himself for it. Despite the challenges surrounding him, Atharva began to feel a sense of improvement and recovery.

Atharva, weary from his journey, found his sleeping area on the train and carefully arranged his belongings to create a comfortable space.

For the first time in what felt like ages, he lay down and drifted into a deep, peaceful sleep.

The gentle rocking of the train and the rhythmic clatter of the tracks became a lullaby.

But this tranquillity was shattered by a deafening noise, a cacophony of screeching metal and splintering wood. In an instant, the train was derailed, crashing and tumbling into chaos.

Miraculously, Atharva's compartment was spared the worst of the destruction.

Dazed, he could hear the horrifying symphony of cries, screams, and the death of dreams as passengers grappled with their sudden, violent reality.

Panic set in, and people rushed to escape the twisted wreckage.

Atharva felt paralysed, his mind struggling to process the catastrophe around him. The sunrise cast a faint glow, revealing the extent of the devastation. Shouts pierced the air, urging for help. "Come here and help, boy!" someone yelled, snapping Atharva out of his stupor.

In a state of shock, Atharva stumbled out of the train.

Amid the chaos, he witnessed a monk moving with purpose, helping the injured with a serene determination.

His eyes then fell on a blind man Atharva had met earlier in the journey.

Despite his blindness, the man was making extraordinary efforts to rescue others, using his stick to locate and pull out those trapped.

His acute hearing guided him to the cries for help, proving his disability did not render him helpless.

Atharva watched in awe as the blind man worked tirelessly, his actions defying his limitations. Inspired, Atharva shook off his paralysis and began to assist the survivors.

The scene around them was growing increasingly dire, the wreckage settling into a grim reality.

But amid the rising panic, the blind man's courage and determination sparked a beacon of hope.

His unyielding spirit in the face of disaster taught Atharva a profound lesson: true strength lies not in physical ability, but in the resilience and compassion of the human spirit.

As Atharva joined in the efforts to save lives, the magnitude of the tragedy became clear.

Yet, within the horror, he found a renewed sense of purpose, driven by the example of a man who, despite being unable to see, had the vision and courage to act.

The dawn of a new day broke over the wreckage, and with it, a resolve in Atharva's heart to help those around him, proving that in the darkest of times, humanity's light can shine the brightest.

Amidst the chaos, ambulances, fire trucks, and police cars rushed to the scene, their sirens blaring through the smoky air.

Rescuers hurried to pull blood-soaked bodies from the wreckage, placing them onto stretchers and loading them into the ambulances.

The air was filled with the sounds of life and death—cries for help, moans of pain, and the ceaseless wail of sirens.

Atharva stood in the midst of it all, feeling increasingly numb. He couldn't comprehend the scale of the disaster around him.

In his mind, he recalled the words of the monk and the blind man he had met earlier. "Life is very short and definitely unpredictable," they had said.

His eyes then wandered to the army personnel, dressed in crisp uniforms, moving in perfect rhythm.

Their expressions were stoic; their actions precise and unhesitating. Atharva was struck by their seeming emotionlessness, how they followed commands and saved lives with unwavering focus.

Amidst this scene, Atharva noticed a man with a broken hand attempting to salute an army officer.

The gesture was a poignant reminder of respect and resilience. Suddenly, Atharva felt a hand on his shoulder. It was the blind man. "Hey boy, is everything fine with you?" he asked.

Atharva nodded, though his mind was swirling with confusion and awe. The blind man handed him a phone with a long antenna and said, "Call your parents and tell them you're safe."

Atharva took the phone and, in his daze, mistakenly dialled Shruti's number—only to remember they were no longer together. He quickly corrected his mistake and called home.

His parents' voices were frantic with worry, but Atharva reassured them, "I'm fine. I'll call you back." Hanging up, he found himself drawn to the army troops once more.

As he followed them, Atharva felt a deep sense of respect and admiration growing within him.

These soldiers, unfazed by the dangers around them, worked with a calm efficiency.

Their discipline and bravery were inspiring.

Atharva realised that they weren't emotionless; they had simply mastered the art of controlling their emotions to perform their duties effectively.

Looking at the empty rail track and the rising sun, Atharva felt a stirring within his soul.

Perhaps, like the sun, he too could rise anew—stronger and with a purpose. The idea of showing interest in NCC began to take root in his mind.

As he watched the soldiers bring order to the chaos, Atharva felt his own resolve solidify.

His eyes lingered on their disciplined movements, their authoritative commands, and their unwavering dedication.

In that moment, he made a silent vow to pursue a path that would allow him to protect and serve, inspired by the selfless heroes before him.

♥

Chapter Fourteen

The rhythmic tapping of the drill echoed through the training grounds; each beat a pulse that resonated deeply within Atharva.

It was during one of these sessions, while crafting shoes that Atharva felt a burgeoning passion ignite within him for the opportunities the National Cadet Corps (NCC) presented.

He was captivated by the movements, the synchronisation, the posture, and the balance required in the marching practices.

These exercises, coupled with his academic pursuits, brought a new level of discipline and determination to his life.

As Atharva immersed himself in the rigorous routines, he found himself thriving on the challenges they posed.

The structured environment of the NCC, with its emphasis on precision and endurance, seemed to bring out the best in him.

He felt a sense of purpose and direction that he had never experienced before.

The drills became a metaphor for his life, teaching him the value of balance, focus, and unwavering commitment.

Though Shruti still held a special place in his heart, she was no longer the central beat that drove him.

Instead, his heart now marched to the rhythm of the drills; each tap reinforcing his resolve to excel.

The discipline and resilience he developed through the NCC became the new heartbeat of his existence, guiding him towards a future filled with promise and dedication.

Atharva's transformation was profound. The lessons from the NCC drills extended beyond the parade ground, shaping his character and outlook on life.

He learned to approach every challenge with the same precision and determination he applied to his training.

In doing so, he discovered a newfound passion and drive that propelled him forward, embodying the values of the NCC in every aspect of his life.

♥

Chapter Fifteen

Veeru called back urgently, "ATHARVA, ATHARVA, I need your help! I know you're not well, but can I meet you this evening?"

Atharva replied warmly, "You're always welcome, Veeru. Come home."

That evening, Veeru arrived looking stressed. "I know you're aware of the internet situation—the outage across the country. Luckily, we have a patchy internet."

Veeru started international submarine cable systems connecting India to the rest of the world, providing high-speed internet connectivity. ISPs purchase bandwidth from these systems to provide services to their customers.

Atharva motioned for him to take a breath. "Take a moment to calm down."

But Veeru pressed on, "There's failure in the banking system, defence, entertainment, social media—everything is having a hard time. The problem is the lack of coordination among people."

Everyone is playing the blame game. Some say it's the ISP provider; others say it's a router issue, and so on."

Atharva remained composed. "I understand.

I can try coordinating with my department to give you support, but that would only address one dimension of the issue."

Veeru shook his head. "No, Atharva. The government isn't able to provide solutions for everything. I'm here because I need your holistic advice. As a friend, suggest how to tackle the problem."

Atharva nodded thoughtfully.

"I understand. I can't directly come and say, 'Solve the issue,' because, as you know, I have limitations. I'm not well and away from the internet havoc situation at the moment.

But let me give you an example—it's simple."

Veeru listened intently, ready to hear Atharva's perspective and hopeful for a practical solution.

Atharva leaned in, his voice calm and steady. "It's simple, Veeru. Let's take the cinema industry as an example."

These days, the cinema industry is failing due to a lot of issues and a lack of coordination.

There's a blame game going on—some say the hero isn't making movies; others say there's no content, no writers, no subsidies, no leader, no structure, and no audience coming to watch movies.

Each group points fingers, and ultimately, they blame the government because they believe it's the only entity that doesn't care about critics."

Veeru listened intently as Atharva continued, "Everyone has their own issues and perspectives. We have the assembly office, right?"

That's where all the representatives come together to discuss and make policies for the people, usually taking advice from diplomats who might not have a ground-level understanding of the problems."

Atharva paused for emphasis. "Here's what we do: take the assembly hall for a five-day workshop."

Invite five heroes, fifteen producers, fifteen exhibitors, and fifteen distributors similarly from every segment of the cinema industry.

Call them without prior notice to avoid any pre-planned manoeuvres.

Now involve the chief minister, the cabinet, diplomats, and legislative people.

Listen to everyone's stories and debates about why the industry is failing, what the issues are, and where the problems lie.

Broadcast these discussions live so the public can see and understand where the issues are.

After gathering all the insights, draft a policy and implement it immediately."

Veeru nodded, seeing the practicality of the idea.

Atharva finished, "Basically, instead of discussing with elected representatives who might be out of touch, get the ground-level people and have a direct discussion."

You can apply the same approach to the internet outage issue. Gather everyone into the assembly, televise the debates, and involve the public through polls.

Let the people also decide what they need. This way, you get a holistic view and a better chance at effective solutions."

Veeru smiled and said, "That's a really good and practical approach, Atharva."

As Veeru prepared to leave, Atharva smiled and replied, "Oh, then we get to see an interesting debate very soon."

♥

Chapter Sixteen

"Daddy, Daddy!" Sana rushed towards Atharva with a frustrated yet endearing puppy face, seeking his attention.

She plopped down beside him, blinking her eyes and stretching out her hand to make herself comfortable.

Slowly, like stretching a confession made of bubble gum, she began, "You know what, Daddy? You're not a sweet father. You don't spend time with me at all, don't listen to me at all!"

Atharva could only nod, feeling cornered by her words.

Sana noticed his indifferent nodding, hit her forehead in exasperation, and said, "See, you prove me right every time!" She turned away, sulking.

Atharva lifted her gently and said, "Tell me what you want and be the sugar-free bubble gum."

She turned back with a smile and said slowly, "You know, in my class, they were talking about the Northern Lights, and I want to see them. Please, let's go, Daddy."

You know I'm not allowed to travel, but Daddy, you're a soldier—you can do anything.

And it's not like we're going to war; it's just a vacation to chill."

Atharva nodded, taking in her excitement, but didn't make any commitments.

♥

Chapter Seventeen

Norway, a country renowned for its Northern Lights, offered the perfect weather conditions to witness this natural wonder.

At the Norway airport, Sana clutched her small trolley, eager to show she was being a good daughter.

Sana, being the shortest among the crowd, was trying to show off her physical strength by pulling a trolley that was half her size, filled with only a few drawing books and stationery.

"I'll draw the Northern Lights," she declared enthusiastically. The next minute, she turned to her father, "Daddy, don't you think the page is not enough to draw the Northern Lights? It's a huge sky with so many galaxies."

Atharva didn't answer, but Sana continued, "Daddy, see my hand. It's become red from pulling the trolley," subtly hinting for him to carry it.

She put on a puppy face to convey her plea.

At the airport, Sana tried to pull Atharva to every shop.

"Come, see! It's so beautiful; they've built a shop in the shape of a yellow butterfly. Come, let's go!" She had boundless energy, filling a basket with chocolates and tiny toys.

She came across a small, fair boy who watched her, captivated by her energy as she filled the basket.

Sana politely ignored him, adding a touch of attitude to show she could pull the basket to the billing centre herself. "See, in five minutes, it's red again on my hand," she pointed out.

Seeing her tiny hands struggling, Atharva took the basket from her.

As he did, a lady approached the fair boy, trying to drag him away.

Atharva felt a familiar fragrance and looking up, he realised it was Erica.

♥

Chapter Eighteen

Recalling joint exercises between Norway and India, Atharva said it aloud,

"Atharva," someone pronounced his name differently, with low confidence in her voice. It was clear that she wasn't from India.

A big smile spread across Erica's face as she said, 'Do you remember? You called me the same way the first time!'

You did!!

"Both of them laughed, holding cups of coffee, reminiscing about the good old days."

Sana had already hinted to Atharva about the peaks of her only-child syndrome.

She often expressed her feelings in subtle ways, seeking his attention and affection.

♥

Chapter Nineteen

Ah, the memories of the good old days! As Atharva looked at Erica, he couldn't help but be drawn back to the first time their paths crossed.

Her eyes seemed to ask, *"Do you still find me as beautiful as the day you first saw me?"*.

He smiled, caught in the moment, and thought, *"Let me revisit those feelings and see what my heart whispered about you back then."*.

Recalling Joint exercise, Atharva turned slowly towards the voice which was soft as butter and saw Erica, who was facing the other direction and treating patients.

She wore a white coat and had a stethoscope draped around her neck.

Atharva waited for her to turn towards him, and a beautiful fragrance wafted through the air, making him fall for her even before seeing her face.

When Erica finally turned, her stunning blue eyes, blonde-brown hair, and clear skin captivated him. Her skin looked so smooth; it seemed as if one could easily slide over it.

Atharva found himself mesmerised, simply staring at her.

"Yes, doctor, how can I help you?" he finally responded.

Erica began briefing him about the medical exercise, but Atharva couldn't focus.

As Atharva leaned against the wall, letting the night air calm him, something—or rather, someone—captured his attention.

There she was, dressed in an elegant outfit with a delicate white coat, moving with a grace that seemed almost otherworldly.

Her dark, defined eyebrows framed eyes that spoke of depth; their softness reminiscent of a gentle deer.

Every glance she cast across the room was deliberate; her presence so commanding that Atharva couldn't look away.

How can someone be so flawless? he wondered, his breath catching. Her skin seemed to glow under the golden lights, smooth and radiant, yet it was her authenticity that drew him in.

She wasn't overly polished or artificial; she was real.

There was something poetic about the way she carried herself—even her clumsiness, which she had casually mentioned with a soft laugh, seemed endearing to him.

As she moved gracefully through the crowd,

Atharva's thoughts spiralled. *God, how could you create someone so breathtaking and expect me not to notice? Yet, a* voice in his head reminded him, *She's out of your league, Atharva.*

Let it go. But his heart rebelled. *Even if I can't have her, I'll cherish this moment, like admiring the fleeting beauty of the stars.*

In the sea of heavily made-up faces, she stood out like the moon among stars. She radiated simplicity and elegance, her dress flowing perfectly, her demeanour calm and composed.

She wasn't just beautiful; she was magnetic.

"Who is she?" Atharva whispered to himself, his pulse quickening.

"She's too beautiful for me," he muttered, doubting himself. Still, his heart followed her every step.

The soft light illuminated her face as she moved, highlighting her expressive eyes and graceful walk.

He noticed the subtle click of her heels, laughing internally at his own thought:

She's not taller than me; it's just the heels—and her presence.

When she turned a corner, panic set in.

How will I find her again in this exercise? He thought. Desperation took over, and he followed the faint sounds of laughter, hoping they would lead him to her.

And then he heard it—a voice calling out her name. "Erica, not that way!" She turned her head, and Atharva's heart leaped.

Erica, Her name was music to his ears. He stayed rooted in his spot, too nervous to approach, content to steal glances as she walked away.

It was as if the screen itself had been designed to frame her beauty.

The soft, fresh glow of her skin seemed to radiate warmth, and *"Afreen Afreen"* began playing in his mind as if the universe conspired to describe her.

Her chin was a masterpiece in itself—delicate, perfectly contoured, a touch of elegance that felt too divine for words.

Soft pink hues complemented her skin like a colour born solely to adorn her. "Pink," Atharva thought, "must have been discovered after someone saw it on her."

This time, her face filled his screen, framed by a simple black top.

Her expressions were a canvas of emotion, each more captivating than the last. Her wide, expressive eyes moved with thought, her lips curving upward in a smile that revealed a rare dimple at its edge.

Each gesture, each tilt of her head, seemed to narrate a story only she could tell.

Her beauty wasn't just skin-deep; it was a symphony of details, from her tired yet twinkling eyes to the blush that danced across her cheeks.

He wished he could pause her face to capture a single moment to save for his dreams, but her beauty was ever-changing, like a kaleidoscope.

Her long, flowing hair reminded him of a fairytale – a tower and a prince climbing up to reach his love.

"Perhaps I should climb her balcony instead," he joked silently to himself; her every move now etched in his mind as a treasure to replay when the world went quiet.

Atharva sighed, his heart full yet longing for more. Under the blanket, he whispered, "I'll be your prince, Erica, for all the days to come."

And with her image still vivid, he drifted into dreams where her beauty painted the skies.

Atharva stood there, a mix of emotions swirling within him as the memories flooded back.

It had been such a fleeting week—a joint exercise that should have been just another routine task in his life. Yet, it wasn't.

It was the moment he met Erica, the woman who would redefine his understanding of beauty, grace, and love.

She was the prefix to his limitless love. In a very short joint exercise of a week, he had fallen for her!

To Erica, with Love from lost Atharva

In the green woods where we played, I let you win,

Just to see your joyous, victorious grin.
But you, with kindness, gave me a turn,
A lesson in love, a heart to discern.

Money spent on whims, I argued with pride.
You showed me how to save, with patience as your guide.
When rain soaked my notes and left me in dismay, You
stepped in with confidence, saving the day.

In the Himalayas, where breaths were few,
You shared your oxygen, your courage shining through.
"I'm from high altitudes, I can manage," you'd say. Your
selfless love guided me on my way.

At base camp, where my voice would falter and break,
You spoke for me, for our future's sake.
Where I felt so small and misplaced, You bridged the
gap, gave me confidence and grace.

Your expressions, a canvas, ever so bright;
From childlike wonder to calm in the night.
You turned my chaos into organised calm,
With you, I found my strength, my charm.

No matter your look—clumsy hair or sleepy face,
You always attracted me with natural grace.
Memories of training, where I was the last,
Your lily's fragrance brings the past.

Lighting lamps at sunset, an agent of light;
Your presence banished the dark of night.
In exercises, lifting you high,
Together, we'd soar, touching the sky.

Erica, my love, in every glance and sigh,
I cherish you more as time goes by.
With each word, each moment, my heart does proclaim,
In the book of my life, you're the sweetest refrain.

Since Erica also had an interest in Atharva, she
agreed to meet him for a night walk.

♥

Chapter Twenty

The beach streets lay empty, shrouded in a cold, persistent wind that seemed to echo with whispers of untold stories. Erica stood by her window, holding a vibrant sari in her hands.

Glancing at the note Atharva had sent—a simple request to meet at the end of the street where the church bells rang faintly in the distance.

Tonight, she decided to leave behind her usual uniform and wear something different, something special. She wanted to impress Atharva.

As the glass of wine in her hand emptied, she felt her nerves loosen, though her heart still fluttered with anticipation.

Slipping into the saree, she adjusted its intricate folds repeatedly, feeling both exhilarated and self-conscious.

The vibrant colours and delicate patterns danced in the wind, making her look like a fleeting vision of elegance against the grey, desolate street.

At the other end of the lane, Atharva waited. He, too, had shed his usual appearance, donning a Western suit that felt unfamiliar yet fitting for the occasion.

He clutched a small bouquet of roses—red, fresh, and fragrant.

The first blooms of his garden felt symbolic, a gesture as delicate and meaningful as the moment itself.

The wind carried Erica's fragrance towards him, mingling with the cool, crisp air.

As she approached, Atharva's heart raced, his eyes fixed on her. The sari's flowing fabric seemed to defy the wind, framing Erica in a way that left him momentarily breathless.

Erica, equally captivated, noticed Atharva's sharp suit and the roses in his hand.

The unexpectedness of his appearance made her smile nervously, her cheeks tinged with red from the cold and perhaps, something more.

The wind played its mischievous role, tugging at Erica's sari and Atharva's coat tails, intertwining their worlds before they even spoke.

"These are for you," Atharva said, stepping closer and holding out the bouquet.

The roses' vibrant red seemed to defy the muted tones of the street.

"I wanted to bring something as beautiful as you are today."

Erica's heart skipped a beat as her fingers brushed against his while accepting the roses.

"Thank you, Atharva. You look… different. Good difference," she added, her smile widening as she took in the sight of him.

"And you," he replied, his voice soft yet sincere, "I've never seen you in traditional attire. It's stunning."

For a moment, they stood in silence, simply marvelling at each other.

The distant church bells rang again, a gentle reminder that time was still moving, though it felt as if the world had paused just for them.

Atharva extended his hand, his fingers brushing hers before gently entwining them. "Shall we?" he asked, gesturing towards the path ahead.

Erica nodded, a newfound warmth dispelling the cold around them.

Side by side, they began walking down the empty beach, the wind their only companion, their hearts beating in quiet unison.

Far away, in the vast expanse of the ocean, Erica stood staring at the waves, each crest and fall a reflection of her own uncertain thoughts.

On the other side of the sea, Atharva found himself aboard an imaginary ship, navigating waters without a clear destination.

They never spoke of the past or speculated about the future; instead, they lost themselves in the present—feeling the air, tasting the wind, and breathing in the scent of each other.

Their silences were not empty but full of words they didn't yet know how to say.

As their steps drew them closer, the space between them seemed to waver.

Their eyes locked, their breaths synchronised, and their lips edged nearer.

As the golden hues of the sunset faded into the horizon, he gently cupped her face, their lips meeting in a tender kiss.

His hands slipped to her waist, pulling her closer, while her fingers instinctively clutched the fabric of his uniform on his shoulders. Her saree billowed in the gentle breeze, its vibrant colours illuminated by the soft glow of the full moon.

Behind them, the waves crashed rhythmically against the shore, their melody blending seamlessly with the magic of the moment.

Together, they stood entwined, a silhouette of love framed by the celestial harmony of moonlight and ocean whispers.

Yet, something unspoken held them back— a lingering doubt, a silent tug of differing thoughts that felt like an invisible chasm.

In that suspended moment, as they hovered on the brink of something profound, the first light of dawn broke across the horizon. The sunrise painted the world in hues of gold and pink, a quiet reminder that each new day held its own promise.

♥

With the cool breeze rustling gently around them, Erica reached into her bag and pulled out a folded piece of paper.

She handed it to Atharva, her eyes sparkling with a hint of mischief and mystery.

"Open it when you're back at the camp," she said softly, her voice carrying the weight of something unsaid.

Atharva took the letter, his fingers brushing hers briefly.

He nodded, though his curiosity flared. Erica smiled faintly, turned, and walked away, her sari swaying in rhythm with her steps.

Hours later, as the sun dipped low and painted the horizon in shades of amber, Atharva found a quiet spot away from the world. With the wind whispering around him, he carefully unfolded the letter.

The faint scent of her lingered on the paper, and his heart raced as he began to read the words she had left behind.

♥

My Dearest Atharva,

As the sun rises and sets, marking the passage of time, so too must we acknowledge the shifting tides of our lives.

Our love, a delicate flower, has bloomed brightly despite the shadows of distance and the echoes of our differing dreams. But now, my heart must pen these words, like petals falling from a once-vibrant bloom.

The miles that stretch between us are not merely of the earth but of the soul. Our paths, though beautifully entwined for a time, diverge like rivers seeking their own course.

The compass of my heart trembles, knowing that love cannot always conquer the expanse that lies between our worlds.

We are like the sun and moon, sharing the same sky but destined to travel our own orbits.

Your dreams are stars that shine brightly, guiding you towards horizons I cannot follow. My own dreams, though equally luminous, chart a course that leads away from you.

Our hearts have danced to a symphony of passion and understanding, yet the notes of our differences play a discordant tune. In the quiet moments, I hear the whispers of reality, reminding me that love, as powerful as it is, cannot bridge the chasm of our opposing views.

So, my love, with a heart heavy with sorrow and gratitude, I must let you go. Know that every moment we share will be a cherished memory, a treasure of the heart.

Our love was a fleeting season, beautiful and profound, but now the time has come for us to part ways. May the winds of fate carry you gently, and may your path be illuminated by the dreams you hold dear. Though we cannot walk this journey together, your spirit will forever dance in the garden of my heart.

With all my love,

Erica ♥

His hands trembled slightly as the faint scent of her lingered on the paper. The poetic cadence of her words filled his mind, and he realised, with a pang in his chest, that it was a goodbye.

Her words, though tender, spoke of distance and parting, of paths that diverged.

Yet, as the ache settled in, Atharva's lips curled into a faint smile.

He whispered softly to himself, the determination in his voice unwavering, *"I will do it. I will make her fall in love with me again."*

He sat on the edge of a cliff, where the relentless tides crashed against jagged rocks below.

The sea stretched endlessly before him, vast and timeless, its every movement mirroring the storm within him.

The advancing waves seemed to bring with them a fleeting sense of hope and joy, a reminder of Erica's presence and the love they once shared.

But as the waves retreated, they carried with them his happiness, leaving a void, an ache that echoed his longing for her.

Atharva gazed at the horizon, his thoughts swirling like the turbulent waters below.

He knew their journey had been fraught with misunderstandings and unspoken fears, yet the love they had shared was undeniable.

It was a force as vast and unyielding as the sea before him.

"If the waves can erode even the mightiest rocks over time," he thought, "Then can my love bridge the distance between us."

He resolved to confront the misunderstandings that had created a rift between them, to fight for their love with the same persistence as the tides that never ceased their dance with the shore.

The wind picked up, carrying with it the salty tang of the sea. Atharva closed his eyes, letting the breeze brush against his face as if it were Erica herself caressing him with her memory.

In that moment, he made a silent promise to the ocean and to himself: no matter the challenges, no matter the distance, he would fight to win her heart again.

With the sea as his witness, Atharva rose from the cliff's edge, his resolve unshakeable.

This wasn't an ending – it was a new beginning. One where love, no matter how battered by the tides of time, would find its way back to the shore.

Chapter Twenty-One

In a small coastal town where the sea whispered secrets to the cliffs lived Arjun, a kind-hearted young man known for his unwavering optimism.

Arjun and Maya, who had fallen in love, were struggling to overcome the unique challenges their blindness presented in their relationship.

Arjun, a talented musician, and Maya, a gifted sculptor, had met at a local art exhibition.

Their connection was immediate, as if their souls recognised each other even before their hands did. However, the obstacles they faced seemed insurmountable.

They found it difficult to navigate their surroundings together, leading to frequent misunderstandings and moments of frustration.

Atharva, moved by their plight and inspired by his own unyielding hope, decided to help them find a way to be together.

He invited them to his favourite spot on the cliffs, where the tides constantly crashed against the rocks, creating a symphony of nature's resilience.

As they sat on the cliff, Atharva began to speak. "Arjun, Maya, love is like these tides."

It can be powerful and relentless, but it can also ebb and flow. The key is to find a way to ride the waves together."

He proposed an idea: "Instead of focusing on what you can't do, let's find ways to amplify what you can do together."

Arjun, your music is your voice to the world. Maya, your sculptures are your hands speaking in the language of art. What if we combine these gifts to help you navigate life together?"

Atharva spent weeks with them, teaching them how to communicate through their art.

The rhythmic sound of the waves provided a serene backdrop for his plan.

"Okay, Maya," Atharva began, his voice gentle yet encouraging, "I want you to learn the chords of Arjun's guitar."

Arjun, you'll write the chords on the beach sand, and Maya, you'll use your sense of touch to read them. Let nature be the cure for your challenges."

Maya, with a beautiful voice that could captivate anyone, smiled at the suggestion. "And Maya," Atharva continued, "can you sing along with Arjun's guitar? Let your voice blend with his music."

Maya nodded, her heart brimming with determination. She crouched down, running her fingers over the sand as Arjun carefully etched out the guitar chords.

She traced the lines, feeling the shapes and patterns, learning to interpret the music through touch. Arjun, too, felt the words he wrote, ensuring he could guide her accurately.

As they practised, the beach became their sanctuary.

The sound of Arjun's guitar mingled with Maya's voice, creating a harmony that seemed to rise with the tide.

Maya's lyrics, inspired by the melodies, flowed effortlessly.

She began to sculpt in the sand as she sang, her hands moulding the grains into shapes that mirrored the songs.

Arjun played his guitar with renewed passion as Maya's sculptures took form, each one a reflection of the music they created together.

Their bond grew stronger with each passing day; their artistic collaboration a testament to their love and perseverance.

Under the watchful eyes of the setting sun and the whispering waves, Arjun and Maya found a rhythm that transcended their limitations.

They learned to trust in each other and in the natural world around them, using their unique talents to overcome the challenges they faced.

Atharva, standing a little way off, felt a deep sense of satisfaction.

He had witnessed the transformation of two souls who, through creativity and determination, had turned their drawbacks into strengths.

As Maya sang and sculpted to the chords of Arjun's guitar, their love and art became one, harmonising with the beauty of the sea and sky.

In that magical moment, they knew that together, they could conquer any obstacle. Their love, like the tide, was powerful and enduring, carving a path through the sands of time.

Arjun and Maya stood side by side, holding hands.

They had learned to navigate their world together, using their unique talents to overcome their limitations.

The tides below crashed against the rocks, but instead of feeling fear or frustration, they felt a profound sense of unity and accomplishment.

He knew that their journey had only just begun, but they were now equipped with nature and the confidence to face whatever challenges lay ahead.

The love between Arjun and Maya was like the sea – boundless, powerful, and enduring.

As they walked away from the cliff, guided by the music and the touch of their art, Atharva felt a sense of fulfilment.

He had shown them that with creativity, perseverance, and a little help from a friend, even the greatest obstacles could be overcome.

And in doing so, he reaffirmed his own belief in the transformative power of love and hope.

Arjun and Maya became the talk of the town for their unique way of loving each other.

The public was inspired by their relationship, and their story gained even more attention when the chief editor of a leading French magazine witnessed their special bond.

The editor published an article titled "Love is Not Blind, For the Blind," celebrating their extraordinary love.

♥

Chapter Twenty-Two

Atharva quickened his pace, eager to surprise Erica with a magazine article featuring Arjun and Maya. As he reached the base camp, the place buzzed with activity, everyone preoccupied with packing. His eyes scanned the familiar surroundings until he spotted the usual campfire spot where Erica often waited.

Just as he was about to reach her, a trainee's urgent call halted him in his tracks. "Sir, you've been called to the office!"

Suppressing a sigh of frustration, Atharva changed direction and made his way to the office. His expression remained impassive, though inside, he felt a gnawing sense of unease. The front office lady greeted him with a polite nod. "Please wait for ten minutes; the head of the exercise will see you shortly."

The minutes dragged by, each second amplifying the tension in Atharva's chest. When he was finally ushered in, the head wasted no time getting to the point. "Atharva, you're suspended until further notice. There's an ongoing investigation concerning you."

Atharva blinked, stunned. "Sir?" he managed, his voice barely above a whisper.

The head's tone softened slightly. "On the night you were on duty guarding the weapon section, a gun went missing. You were responsible for the logbook and security that night. Until we conclude the investigation, you'll need to step aside. I'm sorry, Atharva. We trust your integrity, but protocols must be followed."

A heavy silence settled in the room. Atharva couldn't muster a response. He nodded stiffly, turned on his heel, and left. The world outside felt different now, colder, harsher. Erica noticed him from afar and hurried over, concern etched on her face. "Is everything okay?" she asked breathlessly.

Atharva tried to compose himself, but the weight of the situation bore down on him. "Nothing, Erica. See you soon. Take care," he mumbled before walking away.

Unwilling to let him go without comfort, Erica caught up to him. Her hand rested gently on his shoulder, her voice soft yet firm. "You are my shadow, my triumph, my kin. In the rain, you are my shelter—always near, always the soul who cares for me."

Atharva gave a weak smile but couldn't find the strength to respond.

Back in his room, he began packing his belongings.

Removing his uniform for what felt like the last time, he was hit by a painful memory – the same hollow feeling he had experienced during his school suspension years ago.

His fingers trembled as he folded the fabric, each movement deliberate, weighed down by sorrow.

Dragging his bag behind him, he made his way towards the gate.

The world around him blurred as dizziness overtook him. His breath came in shallow gasps.

He stumbled forward, legs giving way beneath him, until finally, he collapsed. The gate seemed so close, yet impossibly far.

Strong hands grabbed him, dragging him to a corner. As his vision cleared, he realised he was surrounded by several men—Erica's batchmates.

They weren't in Indian Air Force uniforms. Before he could react, the first blow landed, followed by another. They beat him mercilessly, the pain searing through his body.

He realised too late that his drink had been spiked earlier.

Barely conscious, Atharva caught a glimpse of Erica. Dressed in a white coat, she rushed to his side, her face pale with worry.

She knelt beside him, gently caressing his forehead, her fingers brushing through his hair. Her touch was a balm, soothing the physical and emotional wounds.

"You're alright, Atharva," she whispered, pressing a soft kiss to his lips. "I'm so sorry for what happened. I brought you to a private hospital. They're running tests on the substance in your drink."

Atharva locked himself in his room afterwards, overwhelmed by the storm of emotions—the suspension, the betrayal, Erica's pain.

He broke down, tears streaming down his face. Amid the chaos, he found an old letter from Shruti in his bag. Attached was a short note from Erica: "Please take care."

His heart ached with the weight of the message. Days turned into weeks, and each passing moment felt like an eternity. Every job application he sent out came back with a rejection.

He vividly recalled one day when, after his third interview at the same company, he was rejected yet again. Standing in the pouring rain, he had no money to get home. Overwhelmed, he sat on the sidewalk, tears blending with raindrops, the sting of failure cutting deep.

Confusion and frustration plagued him. Was he underqualified or overqualified? The answer remained elusive. A small ray of hope emerged when he secured a job training at a gym.

It wasn't much, but it allowed him to survive. Slowly, a fierce determination began to build within him—a burning desire to achieve something greater. He realised that failure wasn't the end; it was a push towards a path meant for him, one that demanded resilience.

Even as life continued to test him, Atharva found strength in his belief that success was about making the right decisions at the right time, not mere luck.

Yet, just as he was beginning to find his footing, Erica sent him a letter. Her words cut deeper than any rejection: "Atharva, we don't belong to the same community or country. We need to end this."

Atharva couldn't accept it. The bond they shared felt too profound to be dismissed over such reasons.

He knew Erica wasn't speaking her heart. Despite his efforts to reach out, she shut him out completely. Days later, he saw her at an ice cream shop, laughing with her friends. Hoping for closure, he approached her, but her carefree smile told him everything. She had moved on.

At that moment, Atharva understood a painful truth—once a girl decides to leave, she never comes back. He knew he had to distance himself from people and channel his pain into something meaningful.

Finding solace in the belief that everything happens for a reason, Atharva began to see life's grand design. Slowly, Gayathri Shruti entered his life, offering hope when he was at his lowest. Her presence reminded him that when something bad happens, something good is sure to follow.

Though Erica had moved on, Atharva harboured no ill will. He wished her well, believing that letting go of anger was essential to finding peace. He trusted that the universe would balance everything out in time.

Controlling his emotions, he focused on moving forward, knowing that life would reward him for his endurance.

Atharva resolved to keep pushing forward, trusting that the gifts meant for him would arrive when the time was right.

Until then, he would hold his breath and continue the journey, believing that every setback was shaping him into the person he was destined to become.

♥

Chapter Twenty-Three

As Erica and Atharva finished their conversation at the airport, their coffee mugs now empty, they transitioned to sipping beer from jugs. Their kids were sound asleep nearby.

Atharva leaned in and shared his plan to see the Northern Lights.

Erica, with a hopeful smile, asked, "Can I join you both?"

Atharva replied, "Of course!" Then, with a curious glance, she added, "By the way, I've been meaning to ask you—what happened next after we broke up?"

Atharva nodded, intrigued. "Sure, I'll tell you the whole story."

Atharva tightened his grip on the steering wheel, the cold wind whipping through his hair as he drove the open-top car through the snow-covered roads of the Northern Hemisphere.

Beside him sat Erica, bundled up in a thick coat and scarf, her cheeks pink from the cold.

In the back seat, their children were snuggled under a warm blanket, sound asleep, their peaceful faces illuminated by the faint glow of the dashboard lights.

As they drove through the picturesque landscape, Atharva's mind drifted back to the tumultuous events that had led them here.

Atharva said, "I lived under a cloud of suspicion. I felt isolated and anxious, unsure of what the future held."

One day, Atharva was at home. He received a call from his superior. "Atharva, we've completed the investigation," the officer said. "You've been cleared of all charges."

Relief flooded through him. "What happened?" he asked.

"It turns out one of the senior officers was trying to smuggle the weapon out to settle a personal vendetta," the superior explained.

"He manipulated the records to make it look like you were responsible. He said you will receive the confirmation letter via post."

Atharva was reinstated, but the experience had left a lasting impact on him.

Determined to move forward and rebuild his life, Atharva decided to take Air Force exams for a higher authority position in a different cadre.

It was his way of fighting back, regaining control over his career, and proving that despite the hardships, he could still rise above the challenges.

The road stretched out before them, a ribbon of white cutting through the snow-covered landscape.

Atharva's thoughts returned to the present as he glanced at Erica again.

Atharva spent countless hours poring over books, taking practice tests, and attending coaching classes.

It was a gruelling process, but he was determined to succeed.

After months of hard work and dedication, the results were finally announced.

Atharva had passed the exam with flying colours. It was a moment of triumph and celebration for the entire family.

But with success came a new set of challenges.

Atharva was posted as an Air Commodore.

He felt like the happiest person in the world. Putting on a cap, he stepped out and walked toward the market near his house, overwhelmed with emotion.

Tears of joy streamed down his face as he moved through the crowd, even though no one seemed to notice him.

He had an urge to scream to the world, "Yes, I did it!" The sense of accomplishment filled him, and for the first time in a long while, he stood confidently among the people, feeling proud of himself.

"Let me take the risk and move forward," he thought, determined to face whatever came next.

As they drove further north, the sky began to change. Hints of green and purple started to appear, dancing across the horizon. The Northern Lights were beginning to make their appearance.

"Look," Sana whispered, pointing towards the sky. "It's starting."

Atharva pulled the car over to the side of the road, and they all got out, wrapped in blankets and coats.

They stood in awe as the sky transformed into a breathtaking display of colours. Sana's eyes were wide with amazement.

"This is incredible," Atharva said, his voice filled with awe. "I'm so glad we made this trip,"

Sana nodded, her eyes shimmering with tears of joy. "It's more beautiful than I ever imagined."

As they watched the Northern Lights, Atharva reflected on his journey.

The Northern Lights continued to dance above them, casting a magical glow over the snowy landscape.

The children, still mesmerised by the lights, hugged their parents tightly. "This is the best adventure ever," they exclaimed.

Atharva laughed, lifting his daughter into his arms. "And it's only the beginning," he said, looking up at the sky.

Erica glanced at Atharva as they drove through the serene, snow-covered landscape.

♥

Chapter Twenty-Four

"Atharva, I'd like to know about Gayathri Shruthi," Erica inquired with curiosity and open eyes.

Atharva took a deep breath and began, "Shruthi was my schoolmate, and we were deeply in love.

But things didn't work out, and I had to leave school due to pressure from her parents.

We were forced to stay away from each other."

He paused, reflecting on the past. "After being suspended from the Air Force, I spent my days at home, trying to figure out my next steps."

Atharva's voice softened as he continued, "One day, I found out about an event at a mutual friend's house. I decided to go, hoping Shruthi would be there."

"As she neared, she burst into tears and quickly walked away, hiding in a room. I followed her, and when I entered the room, she hugged me tightly and cried for a very long time.

I didn't know whether to hold her or let her go.

She had pushed me away, but in that moment, I realised that sometimes when someone pushes you, it's because they want you even more."

As she stood near me, I felt an overwhelming urge to both hug her and push her away.

My mind was a whirlwind of emotions. Why was Shruthi, after all this time, looking at me now? Why didn't she make any effort to check on me before?

A mix of anger and confusion boiled inside me, but as she held me tighter, I could feel myself softening.

Yet, deep down, I couldn't forget the past. I was the one who got thrown out of school for liking her, who left everything behind for her. And now, here I was, torn between wanting to be with her and the bitterness of those memories.

But inside, I was struggling, unable to fully accept her, still haunted by the unresolved feelings that lingered within me.

The moment I saw her, all I wanted was to pour out everything – the good, the bad, the pain.

But I got lost in her eyes, just standing there, trying to heal her pain.

Atharva gently says, "In the quiet depths of my soul, I was but a speck of dust on your slipper, Shruthi."

And yet, you've let me find a place in your eyes—a place that brings tears, a silent testament to love's enduring power, even amidst life's unpredictable rhythms."

With a soft smile, Shruthi responds, "There may be no steady flow, no perfect tune in the songs you sing, Atharva.

But perhaps that's not what I seek. Instead, be my partner, my strength—a part of me. Together, we can find harmony, even in the imperfections, as love weaves its own music through us both."

Atharva smiled softly and said, "I know emotions are ever-changing, Shruthi. And maybe you're the very storm that stirs them. But perhaps you forget—I'm just a simple lover, attuned to the rhythm of your breath, quietly steady.

You're like the sun in a sunrise, and I'm the shadow that lingers on the land. How do we make this work, you and I? Whether we blend together or remain apart, just stay by my side, Shruthi.

Imagine if this storm could transform into a beautiful melody in our lives."

He paused, his gaze deep with feeling.

"You know how dark it gets down here, where no sunlight reaches. I don't just want to get the light in the day, Shruthi — I want your light, even through the night."

Lowering his voice, Atharva began telling Erica, "But you know what, Shruthi slowly turned into my strength and willpower in my day-to-day activities.

She lost herself explaining to her parents about us, becoming a rebel for me.

Standing in the sun outside the cricket ground, waiting for a glimpse of me, the girl who cared held a bottle of water.

She felt like the shadow of my protector.

As days passed, and my investigation was still ongoing, we didn't realise how addicted we had become to each other.

Every day, her first message and call was always to me.

At times, it was a bit overwhelming, but she had become an inseparable part of my life.

She abruptly discontinued her studies, and I never quite understood why.

There were moments when she seemed lost, miserable, as if she missed me terribly.

Yet, I could sense something more—something was haunting her.

It was as if she was hiding a secret, concealing something from everyone around her."

♥

Chapter Twenty-Five

"But as I was focusing on my exams, I never got a chance to listen to her side of the story or understand her pain," Atharva confessed, his eyes reflecting his regret.

"One day, Shruthi summoned me to her home. I slipped in discreetly, and she led me straight to her bed.

There was no tenderness in her gaze—only a defiant intensity. Bewildered and torn, I followed her lead, unable to grasp what was unfolding.

After we had sex, she silently rose, walked to the kitchen, and sat alone in a corner."

I approached her, asking what was wrong. Her response was a hollow, "Nothing, just forgive me."

I was dumbfounded. "Forgive you? For what? We're fine. Just tell me what's happening."

But instead of answering, she tugged me toward the door, opened it, and said, "Just go. We'll talk later."

I left, reeling from the shock, confusion, and the heavy weight of inexplicable sorrow.

Reluctantly, she had become increasingly rebellious, and I thought she was just idle at home.

But I realised she was slipping into a ghost-like mindset.

Despite this, I couldn't bring myself to truly listen to her.

One day, she fought with her parents and sped off on her two-wheeler at 110 km/h, intent on harming herself.

We argued about her thoughts and actions as she continued to behave abnormally every day.

She would often force me into sex, and I found myself thinking about how the innocent girl I knew in school had turned so rebellious in such a short time.

There was no romance left; she always seemed lost and overthinking about small issues in life."

♥

Chapter Twenty-Six

Then, one day, I got a call from a friend, her voice shaky and urgent: "Can you come near Shruthi's house?" I rushed over, my mind racing with all kinds of thoughts but clinging to the hope that everything would be fine once I got there.

But when I arrived, I was met with ambulances, police, and media swarming around her home.

Fear gripped me as I hesitated to step forward, my breath caught in my chest, struggling to make sense of the chaos and the screams echoing around the house.

I walked in with a sinking feeling, fearing the worst. As I went upstairs, I saw her crying all alone, with the police asking her, "Why did you do it?"

My mind went completely blank. What had she done? What happened? Why is everyone attacking her, dragging her around like this?

I went to hold her, but she refused and pushed me away.

I asked the police what had happened, and they told me she had pushed her neighbour from the terrace.

I was in shock, my mind numb, as I watched her being taken away by the police.

The girl who once had so much charm and calmness was now in a helpless state. I just followed the police van.

Her rebellion had taken over, pushing her to extremes that neither of us could have foreseen.

My visits to the police station were met with frustration and sadness. I wanted to help her, to understand what had led to this tragic turn of events, but I felt powerless.

Despite my best efforts, I couldn't shake the image of Shruthi being taken away by the police.

It haunted me day and night, a constant reminder of how fragile our lives had become.

And for me, I resolved to honour her memory by living my life with the same strength and determination she had shown.

♥

Chapter Twenty-Seven

I got a call from the police asking me to come back to the city immediately.

When I arrived, they made me sit down, gave me some water, and said there were two shocking pieces of news about Shruthi.

"After examining her, the doctors diagnosed Shruthi with schizophrenia."

Schizophrenia is a severe mental disorder characterised by profound disruptions in thinking, perception, and emotional responsiveness.

- Hallucinations: Seeing, hearing, or feeling things that are not present. Auditory hallucinations, like hearing voices, are particularly common.

- Delusions: Strongly held false beliefs that are resistant to reasoning or contrary evidence, such as believing one has special powers or is being persecuted.

- Disorganised Thinking.

She had been hearing strange voices that were commanding her to do random things.

She never opened up about it to anyone, and now she urgently needs treatment.

"The second piece of news was even more shocking—she was pregnant, and she hadn't told anyone."

The police explained that judicial custody or any formal inquiry would be very hard on her and against the law, especially considering her condition and the pregnancy.

For the well-being of both Shruthi and the baby, they decided to move her to a safe and secure place.

"I asked if I could see her, but they said it wouldn't be a good idea at that point. With a heavy heart and a lot of pain, I signed the papers and left, feeling completely numb."

On one hand, I was overjoyed at the thought of becoming a father to Shruthi's baby.

But at the same time, her mental state terrified me, fearing that it might push her even further into harm than I had ever imagined.

But the incident where she pushed the neighbour from the terrace left me with a lingering question:

What trauma was she enduring? Did she notice something unusual, or was someone tormenting her?

"Days turned into weeks, and I finally received a call from the medical facility."

They informed me that Shruthi was responding well to the treatment.

The voices had started to fade, and she was showing signs of improvement.

They assured me that she was in good hands and that they were taking all necessary steps to ensure her safety and the baby's health.

I walked into the room and sat down next to Gayathri Shruthi.

As I did, a story of Shiva and Parvati came to mind—the one where Parvati, in her most furious form, was destroying all the demons, embodying the wrath of Kali.

It was only when Shiva arrived, placing a gentle touch on her, that her anger subsided and she returned to her calm self.

At that moment, I realised that Gayathri needed that same touch from me.

She was furious, her emotions raging like a storm. But the instant I reached out and touched her, she softened, and her anger melted away.

Shruthi sat in silence, not even whispering a sound.

She had gained weight from the pregnancy, and I knew it was our baby. I approached her gently, and she kept her head down, looking like a small child, and whispered, "Sorry."

I said, "It's okay," trying to offer comfort.

When I attempted to hug her, she refused. The doctor stepped in, explaining that she was on medication and asked if I could leave soon.

With a heavy heart, I walked out, feeling the weight of our past and her pain.

However, despite the achievement, I found no joy in it.

The memory of Shruthi, her apology, and the sight of her sitting there haunted me. My success felt hollow without her by my side, and the future seemed uncertain and bittersweet.

Erica and Atharva arrived at their planned resting place in Norway for the day.

Atharva gently carried a sleeping Sana to the bed, making sure she was comfortable.

Erica asked, "So, is Sana Shruthi's daughter, your baby?" Atharva softly replied, "Shhhh. Let her sleep."

♥

Chapter Twenty-Eight

Atharva took a glass of whisky and walked out to the balcony, where Erica followed him.

The night was cool, and the city lights shimmered in the distance. Atharva took a deep breath before beginning his story.

"As her delivery went on, I was in training. It was Sana. When I first rushed to see her, I was filled with joy.

I think that was the best moment of my life."

Atharva said, his voice heavy with emotion. "But then, the very next day, Shruthi tried to kill herself with a sharp object.

She was kept in intensive care, and three days later, she was declared dead."

I can hardly believe she attempted to take her own life, but soon, everything began to unfold from her diary and her friends. After I was expelled from school, she was consumed by guilt, knowing she was the reason behind it.

Friends and people around the school blamed her, which led to a gradual descent into depression.

She started hallucinating, imagining that I was there with her, providing comfort.

Her neighbour took advantage of her fragile state, pretending to be me, Atharva. As I re-entered her life, Shruthi slowly began to emerge from her hallucinations, realising that her neighbour was not Atharva.

When he approached her on the terrace, she recognised the truth and rejected him. In the ensuing struggle, he slipped and fell to his death.

Basically, everyone faces problems in life; it's all about seeking out help from people with the right intentions. In a society full of opportunists, this makes all the difference.

Atharva paused, his eyes distant. "I see Shruthi in Sana. I miss her so much."

He started to cry, the pain of his loss evident in every tear. "She gave me Sana as the best memory of my life and then left us all."

Atharva gently handed Erica a folded piece of paper. "Erica," he said softly, "Shruthi wrote this letter before she died.

It's for her baby. Please read it."

When you read this letter, you'll be alive,
A precious soul, a light to thrive.
I pray to God for you, I plead,
May your dreams be vast, as endless as the sea.

Dear God, protect this soul of mine,
From hardships and the cruel decline.
I've taken pain, I've borne the weight,
Let it end with me, seal her fate.

God, please listen with tender care,
Make your plans gentle, kind, and fair.
You did not love me, this I know,
But give my soul your love to show.

Let her hear your music, sweet,
Dance to the rhythm of life's beat.
Take her, God, as your own soul.
Guide her steps like flowing water.

I feel relief, emerging anew,
From life's misdeeds to skies of blue.
Let her lips be sweet like honey.
Her eyes hold galaxies, bright and sunny.

My God, dear God, hear my plea. Let no evil touch her, let her be free.

Erica placed a comforting hand on his shoulder, her heart breaking for him.

After Shruthi left, Atharva would often whisper to himself, *"She was the only one I ever desired in my life, but she's gone now.*

Yet, she remains in every corner of my heart."

His voice would falter as he continued, *"I can only hope she finds her way back to me someday. She wasn't just a part of my life—she was my life. She was the very breath I breathed, the trust I held in the purity of true love."*

"But Sana is like a growing butterfly," Atharva continued. "I don't want her to know much about Shruthi's struggles.

I want to protect her from that pain."

Erica hugged him tightly as he cried.

"You're doing your best, Atharva.

You're giving Sana a loving home, and that's what matters now."

Atharva nodded, though the tears continued to flow.

"Every day, I try to be strong for Sana. She's my everything now."

"You loved her, and you love Sana. That's enough," Erica whispered.

Atharva took a sip of his whisky, staring out into the night.

"Sana has her mother's eyes. Every time she looks at me, I see Shruthi. It's a bittersweet reminder of the love we shared and the pain of losing her." Erica squeezed his hand. "It's okay to feel this way. It's okay to grieve and to miss her. But remember, you're not alone. You have Sana."

Atharva nodded, feeling a glimmer of comfort in Erica's words. "Thank you," he whispered. "For being here, for understanding.

The challenge of legally claiming Sana as my daughter arose, but fortunately, Shruthi's diary detailing our relationship helped me secure my claim."

♥

Chapter Twenty-Nine

The quiet of the night was broken by a soft, fragile voice. "Maa… Maa…" Sana, nestled in her bed, tossed and turned, her little murmurs filled with longing.

Atharva and Erica exchanged a glance, concerned about shadowing their faces. They both moved towards her, their steps cautious and hearts heavy.

Erica reached out first, placing a gentle hand on Sana's forehead. "She's alright," Erica whispered, her voice reassuring as she felt the warmth of her daughter's soft skin.

Sana's eyes fluttered open, and without hesitation, she reached out for Atharva.

"Daddy…" she murmured, her arms wrapping tightly around his neck. He pulled her close, his heart swelling as he cradled her.

"Yes, my angel," he whispered, his voice as tender as his embrace.

Sana buried her face in his shoulder, her voice muffled but clear. "I can't sleep."

Atharva stroked her hair softly, his voice soothing. "It's okay. I'm here."

As she rested her small head against him, she pulled back slightly and looked up. "Where is Maa, Daddy?"

Atharva smiled gently, his eyes warm. "Maa is at home, sweetheart. We'll visit her soon."

Sana's little face scrunched in disappointment. "We should have brought her with us," she insisted, her tone earnest.

Atharva chuckled softly, planting a kiss on her forehead.

Sana sighed, her little body relaxing into his arms, and she soon drifted back to sleep. The innocence and trust in her tiny form filled the room with peace.

Erica, who had been silently watching, broke the silence. "Who is Maa?"

Atharva looked at Erica, his gaze softening. "Maa is my mother," he said simply.

"She raised Sana when she was little, and they're inseparable. Maa spoils her in every way—whatever Sana asks for, she gets."

He paused, a tender smile playing on his lips. "I think she loves Sana even more than she loved me.

She's like a child herself when she's with her granddaughter. I've never seen her so happy."

Erica listened intently as Atharva's voice grew warmer, laced with memories. "When Sana does something good—finishes her chores or helps someone—Maa quietly slips her a few coins. 'This is for your piggy bank,' she'd say, her eyes full of pride."

Sana, he continued, would eagerly place the coins into her little piggy bank, loving the satisfying clink they made.

"But it wasn't about saving for herself. Whenever her piggy bank was full, she'd bring it back to Maa and say, 'This is for you, Maa. I'll take care of you, always!'"

Atharva laughed softly, his heart swelling as he recalled Maa's playful response: "What will I do with all this?"

Sana, undeterred, would puff out her tiny chest and reply with conviction, "You can buy whatever you want!"

He described the simple yet beautiful scenes of their life together—Sana sitting at the dining table, cutting vegetables beside Maa, mimicking her every move.

As they worked, Sana's eyes would grow heavy, her small head eventually resting on Maa's arm. And soon, she'd fall asleep in her grandmother's lap, her soft breaths a melody of peace.

From a distance, Atharva had often watched them, his heart swelling with gratitude.

The love between Sana and Maa was pure and untainted – a love that required no grand gestures, no words.

"Sana once promised she'd take Maa with her when she gets married," Atharva chuckled, his voice tinged with amusement and affection. "I laughed, but I know she meant it."

His tone grew thoughtful. "It's incredible, isn't it? The purity of a child's love. It's free from greed, from ulterior motives. It's just... love. Simple and true."

Erica nodded; her own heart touched by his words.

Atharva continued, his voice low and reflective. "As we grow older, we lose that simplicity.

We get caught up in the world: money, possessions, ambition.

But when I see Sana and Maa together, I'm reminded of what love truly is. It's not complicated. It's not conditional. It just is."

Looking down at the sleeping Sana, he smiled. "It's amazing to watch.

Maa's happy just being part of Sana's journey. There's something magical about the bond between a grandparent and a grandchild. It's a love that melts every barrier."

Erica leaned into Atharva's words, her own heart swelling with warmth as she watched the peaceful scene before her. The love between them all felt unshakeable, a reminder of the power of family and the purity of love.

♥

Chapter Thirty

Atharva turned to Erica, his voice laced with gratitude and reverence.

"Erica, whatever Maa has today—her peace, her joy—it's because of Shruthi. She played an irreplaceable role in Maa's life."

He paused, the weight of a painful memory washing over him. "It was during the time of my exams.

I was already drowning, struggling with everything—life, responsibilities, expectations.

And then, one day, Maa went out to buy groceries. On that ordinary day, tragedy struck. Right in front of her eyes, a bus hit a young student.

She witnessed everything. The shock was unbearable.

She fell into a deep silence, a silence that spiralled into depression.

Over time, she began showing early signs of mild Alzheimer's—losing track of the simplest memories, forgetting moments that made up her life."

Atharva's voice wavered as he continued, his gaze distant.

"Then came the day that shook me to my core. Maa went missing. I was terrified, lost, consumed by fear.

And yet, Shruthi stood unwavering by my side. She helped me find her, and that day, Shruthi taught me a lesson I'll never forget—the true value of family, of a mother.

It made me reflect on everything a mother sacrifices, everything Maa had given for me."

His voice grew steadier, filled with deep emotion.

"A mother… She dedicates her entire existence to her children from the moment they're born.

Nine months of care, giving up her dreams, sacrificing her body, her desires—all so her child can come into this world safely.

Mothers are like Mother Earth, bearing every burden without complaint, giving everything they have to nurture and protect.

They are the ones who hold a family together, the silent backbone of every home.

Fathers may walk away in some stories, but mothers? They stay. They fight. They endure."

Erica nodded slowly, her heart moved by his words.

Atharva's expression softened. "When a girl becomes a mother, something shifts. Her world narrows to her children and family.

She lets go of her ambitions, her personal desires, everything—because her child becomes her everything.

And with that, she begins to reflect her own mother's qualities—her strength, her resilience, her sacrifices. It's selfless in a way no other love could ever be."

He paused, taking a steadying breath before continuing. "When Maa went missing, I feared I'd lost her forever. That thought haunted me—no one could ever replace her.

In a world consumed by self-interest, a mother's love stands apart, pure and unconditional. She is like a candle, burning herself to give light to others."

Erica's eyes glistened with emotion as she listened, her understanding deepening with each word.

"And Shruthi," Atharva said, his voice filled with both admiration and sorrow, "she embodied that same selflessness.

When Maa disappeared, Shruthi sprang into action. She didn't rest. She plastered advertisements all over the city, contacted NGOs, friends, relatives, even temples.

In just one day, she found Maa sitting alone in a park, lost in her own trauma."

His voice softened further. "From that moment on, Shruthi dedicated herself to Maa's care."

She spent every waking hour with her—arranging treatments, practising speeches, rebuilding Maa's world piece by piece. Through Shruthi's relentless love and devotion, Maa finally began to heal. Life started to return to her."

Atharva smiled faintly, his eyes filled with gratitude. "That's why a mother's love is unparalleled.

It's selfless, beyond comparison. And now, out of gratitude for Shruthi's love and sacrifice, Maa has poured all her care and devotion into little Sana.

It's her way of passing on that legacy of love—a bond that can never be broken."

Erica reached out, her hand finding his. "I understand now, Atharva," she said softly. "Love like that—it changes everything."

Atharva nodded, his heart full, the weight of his memories lightened by the love he still carried for the women who shaped his life.

♥

Chapter Thirty-One

Atharva paced restlessly in the hotel lobby, his attention divided between the phone call in his hand and the scene unfolding in front of him.

His gaze shifted, and he noticed Sana sitting at the table, staring blankly at her untouched breakfast.

Her face, usually so full of life, was now a canvas of exaggerated expressions as she fidgeted with her food, clearly lost in her own world.

From the corner of his eye, Atharva couldn't help but raise an eyebrow in amusement at her antics.

Sana caught his look and, with a mischievous gleam in her eyes, mirrored his raised brow with a playful twist of her lips.

Just then, Erica entered the room, her elegant black saree sweeping gracefully around her as she made her way toward them.

Her presence was magnetic, and Atharva's gaze naturally shifted towards her.

She met his eyes and gave him a subtle, playful lift of her eyebrows; her expression full of unspoken understanding.

Atharva's lips twitched in a smile, their silent exchange a dance of familiarity and charm.

Without missing a beat, Erica reached for a balloon from the hotel's birthday decorations and tossed it toward Sana.

The moment the balloon landed in Sana's hands, her tired expression melted away, replaced by a spark of excitement.

Her face lit up as she eagerly batted the balloon to the floor; her earlier lethargy forgotten.

Erica, amused by the transformation, sent a few more balloons her way.

Sana, who had been weighed down by exhaustion just moments before, now seemed to burst with energy.

Her giggles filled the room as she played with the balloons, her joy infectious, her expression shifting from the dull haze of the morning to the pure exuberance of a child rediscovering delight.

It was as if the sunrise had come alive in her spirit.

Later, when the day's excitement wore off, Sana curled up in Erica's lap, her small body falling into an exhausted sleep.

But after a while, she stirred restlessly. Her face twisted in distress as tears welled up in her eyes, and before anyone could react, she began sobbing uncontrollably.

Startled, Atharva rushed to her side, kneeling beside her with panic rising in his chest.

"What happened, Sana?" he asked gently, his voice full of concern. But the little girl could only cry harder, her tears flowing unchecked.

Suddenly, she threw herself into his arms, clinging to him tightly, her sobs growing louder.

Atharva exchanged a worried glance with Erica, both of them confused and unsure of what to do next.

Through her sobs, Sana managed to whisper between breaths, "Daddy… Daddy… in my dream… there were two pigs…"

Atharva gently rubbed her back, his heart aching at the fear in her voice.

"What happened in your dream, sweetheart?" he asked softly, trying to comfort her.

Sana's voice trembled with terror as she continued, "I was with my friend on a school trip, holding her hand.

And then... two black pigs with no eyes... they attacked me... I ran into a room, but they were waiting outside for me."

Her sobs only deepened, her body trembling in his arms. Atharva held her even closer, his own heart heavy with sorrow.

Erica reached out, trying to offer comfort, but Sana clung to Atharva, her small hands grasping at him in desperation.

"Daddy, don't leave me. Don't go anywhere," she whispered, her voice full of fear.

Atharva's heart broke as he kissed the top of her head and whispered softly, "I'm right here, Sana.

I'm not going anywhere," he held her tightly, his arms wrapping around her protectively as she buried her face in his shoulder.

Slowly, the intensity of her sobs began to fade.

Atharva rocked her gently, murmuring soothing words until her breathing finally evened out and her small body relaxed into the safety of his embrace.

Before long, she was asleep again, her fears soothed by the presence of her father, who would never leave her side.

♥

Chapter Thirty-Two

Erica asked if she could fly back to India with Sana and Atharva. Atharva agreed without hesitation.

Once they landed, Erica made it clear she wanted to meet Maa, who was playing a pivotal role in Sana's and Atharva's lives at this point.

Maa, now fully recovered, had thrown herself into counselling, parenting, and mentoring, keeping her mind sharp and occupied.

The moment Sana saw Maa, she bolted towards her, leaping into her arms, covering her with kisses.

Maa embraced her firmly, kissing her back, but it didn't take long before their playful bickering started.

Atharva and Erica stood by, watching the light-hearted scene unfold, amused by the dynamic.

Eventually, Maa turned to Erica with a nod of acknowledgement, offering a warm but composed welcome.

Maa sat down with a thoughtful expression, her voice steady and calm, but tinged with concern as she spoke to Erica.

"I had a young teenage client recently," Maa began, her eyes soft with compassion. "She was a beautiful and charming girl, but despite her outward appearance, her life was in complete disarray."

Erica leaned in, listening closely. "What happened to her?"

Maa sighed. "She was in such a hurry to settle down early, to keep up with the lifestyle she thought everyone else was living.

Social media had become her measuring stick, and she felt this immense pressure to impress her followers, to show that she was successful, living a glamorous life.

But all it did was lead her into trouble."

"How so?" Erica asked, intrigued.

"She had taken on so many debts at such a young age," Maa explained, shaking her head.

"She thought she needed to buy things, to have what others had, and when she couldn't afford it, she took out loans.

And to get out of those loans, she took on even more. It became a vicious cycle, a debt trap."

Erica frowned. "That's awful. It sounds like she was just trying to keep up, but at what cost?"

"Exactly," Maa said. "She was in a rush to achieve everything before she even turned 30, forgetting that life is a marathon, not a sprint.

It's as if she were playing a T20 match, trying to hit every ball out of the park, but life isn't about quick wins."

Erica nodded, relating to the feeling of pressure to succeed early in life. "So, she wanted to make fast money?"

"Yes, she wanted the easy way out," Maa continued.

"She wasn't consistent with anything. One day, she was gambling online; the next, she was starting small businesses, and then she'd try her hand at becoming a YouTube vlogger.

But there was no commitment, no focus on one path.

She was scattering herself across different ventures, hoping that something would work."

"And did anything work?" Erica asked, already guessing the answer.

"No," Maa replied sadly. "Nothing did. She was so busy trying to do everything that she mastered nothing.

Her debt only grew, and soon enough, she was stuck in a financial mess.

It's like the debt traps we talk about with nations, but this is happening to individuals, to young kids.

Microfinance companies are giving loans to teenagers who don't even have the maturity to handle money."

Erica's brow furrowed. "That's so dangerous. Kids aren't being taught how to manage their finances, and they're falling into these traps."

Maa nodded in agreement. "Exactly. Schools don't focus on financial literacy, and social media only amplifies the desire to look successful without teaching the discipline it takes to build something real.

And it's not just about money. Some of these young girls, in desperation to repay their debts, are falling prey to opportunistic men.

They're being sexually exploited by people who take advantage of their vulnerability. It's heartbreaking.

We talk about westernisation like it's a bad thing, but in some ways, they've figured out love and relationships better than us."

Maa gave a small, knowing smile. "Yes, in some ways. While we claim to be modern, many of our values are still confused.

Our young people are lost, unsure of what they truly need.

Even our traditions are being distorted. Arranged marriages, which were once a thoughtful process, have become like a game of chance.

Families pick the 'best card,' hoping it works out, but there's no real love, no honesty."

Erica sighed deeply. "It's true. There's so much focus on appearances and quick success, but no one talks about patience, about the long game."

"Patience is the key," Maa said firmly. "If young people could just slow down, focus on one thing at a time, they would see that they can achieve everything they want in life.

But it takes time, and they have to be willing to wait for it, to work steadily and consistently.

Instead, they're rushing, chasing immediate gratification, and losing themselves along the way."

Erica nodded thoughtfully. "It's like what the Bhagavad Gita says, right? About the three gates to hell—lust, anger, and greed."

"Yes, exactly!" Maa agreed. "These are the traps that lead to self-destruction.

Lust for success, greed for more money, and anger or frustration when things don't go their way.

That's what this girl was caught in—a loop of these three vices.

And if people don't recognise it, they'll continue to spiral down."

Erica leaned back, taking in all of Maa's wisdom. "So what's the solution? How should young people approach life?"

"They need to understand that life isn't a race," Maa said gently. "It's okay to go slow, to take their time.

They need to focus on one goal at a time, give it their full attention, and be patient. Success will come, but not overnight.

It requires dedication, discipline, and time.

If they can do that, they'll avoid the traps and find real, lasting success—not just the kind that looks good on social media."

Erica nodded slowly, her heart heavy with the weight of the conversation but also filled with a sense of clarity. "You're right, Maa.

This really is Kali Yuga. Everything's upside down. But maybe if more people listened, we could turn things around."

Maa smiled softly, placing a hand on Erica's shoulder. "Yes, my dear. It's a difficult time, but with the right mindset, anything is possible. We just have to remember what truly matters in life."

Erica asked, "Mum, is karma the reason for the way children live their lives, or the bad paths they end up following?"

Maa paused for a moment before replying. "It's somewhat connected, Erica," she said thoughtfully.

"But let me share a different example from one of my clients to explain it better. There was a government employee, well-settled in life, who openly admitted that he was deeply corrupt.

He would take money from the poor and needy to get their work done at his desk.

But there was one thing he regretted deeply.

He believed the curses of those people were the reason for his current suffering."

Erica leaned in, curious. "What happened?"

Maa sighed. "He had two children. His eldest son became a drug addict at the age of 16.

He was popping pills, completely out of control.

The father tried everything to get him treated, but the boy was rebellious, out of his senses, and wasted the most productive years of his life.

His health deteriorated, and he was left physically weak."

Erica's eyes widened. "That's terrible."

Maa nodded sadly. "And as if that wasn't enough, his other son was born physically handicapped.

Even though this government employee took all the money he had earned through corrupt means to secure a better future for his children, in the end, his wealth couldn't bring them happiness or health.

His children were in no state to enjoy the life he had tried to provide for them.

He admitted that his bad deeds had come back to him."

Erica sat in silence, absorbing the weight of Maa's words. "So, do you believe the curses of those people and his karma affected his children?"

"Yes," Maa replied. "He realised too late that the wrong he had done had a direct impact on his family.

It's not just about personal karma – it affects your loved ones too. That's why ancestral blessings are so important for future generations.

If you don't keep your conscience and your actions clean, the consequences often fall on the ones you care about most.

In Kali Yuga, those who make mistakes often witness the results of their bad deeds in the same generation through their own loved ones."

Erica listened, her heart heavy with understanding. "So, we really need to keep our books clean, don't we? If not, the ones we love might suffer because of our actions."

Maa nodded solemnly. "Exactly. Karma is not just about individual consequences – it ripples through families and generations. We have to be mindful of the legacy we leave behind."

Maa continued with a soft, reflective tone, "For every parent, their children are their entire world – their dreams, their hopes.

You see, sex isn't just about lust; it's about passing down a soul, creating life.

But I see the younger generation struggling to find a partner, and it's understandable.

They have different expectations now, which is fair.

Yet, when a girl leaves her family to marry a man, trusting him with her life, and he breaks that trust by being swayed by another woman's beauty—how can he truly be a good father to his children, the innocent souls?"

Erica listened intently, her eyes locked on Maa's. Maa continued,

"The same goes for a woman.

If she cannot remain honest in her marriage, if she's drawn to another man after committing to one, how can she nurture her children properly?

Those pure, innocent souls deserve parents who honour their commitments, who lead by example."

Just then, Sana rushed into the room, interrupting their conversation with her usual liveliness.

Erica and Maa both embraced her tightly, a warm, comforting hug that said more than words could.

"This is the best therapy in the world," they both agreed, smiling at the simple joy of love and togetherness.

Maa's voice grew softer, more emotional. "Parents would do anything for their children.

They endure every pain, every hardship, to raise them well. They never say 'no' when it comes to their kids. But as those same children grow up, many start to forget the sacrifices their parents made.

They begin to disrespect them, abandon them. It's heartbreaking, Erica."

Erica nodded, feeling the weight of Maa's words in her heart.

She knew, deep down, that nothing was more precious than the bond between parent and child, a bond built on trust, love, and sacrifice.

And when that trust is broken—by a parent or by the child—it leaves scars on both sides.

Maa said, "The Bhagavad Gita highlights the importance of parents being role models, teaching their children values like honesty and kindness.

It also reminds us that parents should love their children without becoming too attached, as this keeps relationships balanced and healthy.

For parents, nurturing these values is a vital part of their spiritual journey.

When they embody these virtues, they deeply influence the character development of their children.

Kids naturally absorb and reflect these qualities when they see their parents living by them."

♥

Chapter Thirty-Three

Erica asked, "Maa, what is life really all about?"

Maa smiled gently and replied, "What I've shared with you so far, Erica, are the different perspectives people have on life. But if you ask for my own view, you might find it amusing."

Erica tilted her head, curious. "What do you mean?"

Maa chuckled softly. "You see, I believe that everyone needs to fail at some point in life—to experience a free fall.

It's during those moments that Mother Nature steps in to rescue you. But she only comes when you're ready to learn."

Erica listened closely as Maa continued, "Imagine that Mother Nature adopts you, taking on all the pain in your life.

If you evolve with her, she'll always be there to help you rise again. But remember, we don't own her – she is vast, beautiful, and far beyond our control.

Whenever we stumble, Mother Nature nudges us to get back up, pushing us to evolve again."

Maa's voice softened. "Life is colourful, Erica, and Mother Nature is the greatest teacher.

She'll love you when you love and respect your own mother's sacrifices and never forget your father's care. The people who brought you into this world are like gods. And the one who taught you to speak, to communicate, and guided you with principles—your teacher—is also a form of God."

Erica nodded, absorbing every word.

"Whenever you forget life's lessons, Mother Nature will hit you hard, forcing you to learn from your mistakes.

But she'll always give you a chance to be reborn, to start again. That's why you must smile in the face of hardship, for Mother Nature isn't selfish like other people.

She doesn't expect anything in return. She only wants you to keep hope alive."

Maa's eyes sparkled with wisdom as she went on, "Life isn't a race, Erica. It's all about timing. Everything in life may look colourful, but the truth lies in Mother Nature's embrace.

She's the only constant from the moment you leave your mother's womb. So, respect her.

Don't chase after people or money – they are fleeting. Mother Earth is here to help you grow."

"She will rise again like the sun, lift you like the wind, and push you forward like the waves when you're dedicated to your work.

You don't need to run after anything; everything will come to you in time. You just need to be patient."

Maa smiled warmly, her tone soothing. "Nothing in life is permanent—whether it's money, wealth, or respect.

It all fades. What truly matters is living the right way, with a little humanity and good deeds. That's the essence of life."

Erica sat back, reflecting on Maa's words, feeling a deep sense of clarity and peace.

Maa said, "Nowadays, we're spending so much money just to drink the water that Mother Nature provides freely... haha..."

Maa shared another story, "There was a client I once counselled—a highly successful politician who held a prominent position in the cabinet. But by the time I met him, his life was in complete ruins.

You see, when people become very successful, they often attract negative individuals around them—people who shower them with attention, constantly praising them, saying things like, 'You're the greatest.'

And at first, it feels good, but soon, that success starts to go to their head.

This politician started believing he was untouchable, that he could do anything.

His ego grew, and with it came anger and arrogance. He began thinking he was always right, that no one could challenge him.

He became selfish, pursuing power and wealth without considering the consequences.

In his mind, he was above everyone else, and he stopped listening to those who could genuinely help him."

Erica listened intently as Maa continued, "As he got lost in his own sense of importance, he surrounded himself with people who only wanted to benefit from his position and wealth.

The true, honest people—the ones who could have kept him grounded—he pushed them away.

With money and power at his disposal, he thought he could fix any problem, that no mistake was too big to correct.

But that carelessness caught up with him. His ego made him blind, and eventually, his empire crumbled around him.

He lost everything—not because of one big failure, but because he couldn't make even the smallest right decision.

And that's the danger of success if you let it cloud your judgement. Handling power responsibly is the real test."

Erica asked, "Maa, everyone wants success in life. What's the best way to handle it?"

Maa smiled and replied, "There are many ways, Erica. Each person has their own way of managing success, but they stay successful only when they handle it the right way. Let me tell you about Atharva.

Whenever he feels like he's on top of the world, when success overwhelms him, he finds a way to calm himself down.

He takes time off from his busy life and retreats to a farm he owns in the Western Ghats.

There, he spends days alone, away from everything, reconnecting with nature.

He starts by working on the farm, sowing coffee seeds and doing the basic tasks of farming.

He spends time with the soil, the very essence of Mother Earth.

The process is grounding for him. The first step he takes is preparing the soil—loosening and tilling it so that roots can grow deep and breathe.

This reminds Atharva to dig deep into his own life, to reflect on his mistakes and flaws, and to take a breath before moving forward."

Maa continued, "Next, he sows the seeds, planting them in the prepared soil.

He ensures the seeds are healthy and strong, just like how he removes negativity from his life—whether it's bad decisions or the wrong people.

He clears the way for new growth, just like he does with the crops.

Irrigation is the next vital step, ensuring that the plants receive water to grow.

Similarly, Atharva nurtures his mind and spirit with good thoughts, healthy practices, and the right lifestyle, just like a farmer cares for his crops."

Maa smiled as she explained the final part, "And then comes the harvest, where the crops are gathered after they've matured.

Atharva, too, sees the best version of himself emerge, grounded and humble, after his time with the earth. He overcomes the ego that often comes with success.

Mother Earth, through her patient process, allows him to be reborn, helping him evolve. Farmers who've seen the hard work that goes into every crop never waste food.

They respect it. Likewise, Atharva learns to respect the basics of life, understanding the true value of every step."

Erica smiled softly and said, "Maa, I think you're like Mother Nature for Atharva. He can come to you anytime and find the safest, most comfortable place to rest—right there in your lap."

Sana was slowly walking in the garden, keeping a suspicious eye on Erica and Maa from a distance. As she drew closer, she suddenly broke into a run, leaping into Maa's lap.

Maa gently stroked her hair, while Erica, noticing Sana's tired and slightly unhappy expression, asked, "Is everything okay?"

Sana, with her puppy-dog eyes, pulled Erica's hand and pointed towards a mango tree in the garden.

Both Erica and Maa followed her gaze. "I want to have that mango before my holidays end. Can you please pluck it for me?" Sana asked sweetly.

Erica and Maa exchanged a smile and stood up. Instantly, Sana dashed towards the tree, jumping in excitement and calling for them to hurry up.

"This one! This mango! Pluck it!" she exclaimed, bouncing with joy.

Erica reached up to grab one, but Sana quickly protested, "No, not that one—the bigger one!" Maa chuckled and gently reminded her, "That one's not ready yet."

Undeterred, Sana pointed to another side, "Look! This one!"

When the mango was finally in her hands, Sana bolted towards the kitchen, proudly carrying her prized mangoes, her face glowing with happiness.

Sana announced, "I'll slice this squishy mango with my hands," and grabbed a knife with determination.

But as she attempted to cut it, her hand slipped, and she accidentally hurt herself.

In an instant, a sharp cry escaped her lips, and Atharva rushed to her side.

Seeing her in tears, he felt his own emotions well up and started crying too.

Erica moved to comfort him, but his mother gently held her back, whispering, "Let him go through this."

Without a second thought, Atharva scooped up Sana and rushed her to the hospital, his heart aching despite the minor cut on her hand.

This scene touched everyone, especially his mother, who turned to Erica and said, "This is how a man becomes responsible. When the person he loves most is hurt, it shapes him.

Men may hesitate to cry in front of others, striving to appear strong and powerful.

But when it comes to their beloved daughters, they don't think twice about shedding a tear.

Sana has moulded him in ways none of us could, and he would go to any length for her, just as a father should.

He would ignore anyone else telling him to change, but for Sana, he would do anything."

Later, as Sana walked out of the hospital room with a bandage on her hand, she saw Atharva still emotional.

She smiled and said softly, "I'm alright, Daddy," before wrapping her arms around him. Atharva hugged her tightly, unable to hold back his tears.

Watching this tender moment, Erica murmured, "Men may be strong, but with their daughters, they become the most selfless version of themselves."

Maa began, her voice soft but resolute. "Erica, men can seem carefree, as if they drift through life in joy in their adulthood.

But when a man promises his heart, when he chooses a life partner, something profound happens. He's no longer drawn to fleeting desires; he sees the deeper beauty, the divine essence in a woman.

A woman's beauty is not just in her face or form but in her spirit, her grace, and the life she carries within.

You know, Erica, a woman becomes a blessing to the world in a unique way when she brings new life; when she becomes a mother.

In that role, everything changes for her as well. Her world centres around the child she nurtures, a selfless, enduring love.

And a father? He doesn't just love the beauty of his partner;

He feels a whole new depth of love when he holds his child for the first time; a love that's beyond words, beyond sight, for someone he's never even met before that moment.

Men and women may fall in love with each other in the beginning, drawn to each other's beauty, the thrill of attraction.

But together, they grow, and that love deepens as they cherish each other through all of life's colours and seasons.

When children arrive, parents often sacrifice for their little ones, giving up dreams, taking on worries, all to create a safe, loving world for their children.

And it's a hard truth, Erica, that as children grow, they might question or misunderstand the intentions of their parents.

But true joy comes when children, now grown, return that care to their parents, looking after them with the same devotion they once received.

If a parent makes mistakes, it's often because they care deeply; sometimes, the weight of that love can feel like protection that's hard to understand.

The greatest love is not just in romance or passion but in the bond that forms over a lifetime of shared memories, challenges, and the quiet strength of enduring together.

In the end, Erica, it's the star of love that draws us into this grand journey, and the cycle repeats with each generation, an eternal bond that shines in the endless sky of family."

♥

Chapter Thirty-Four

Erica sat down beside Maa, her eyes soft with affection as she asked, "Maa, how is your health these days? Better than before?"

Maa, ever-vibrant, smiled with a hint of pride.

Maa, how is Atharva's health? He's been so restless ever since the bullet wound... It's like he's completely unfazed by the pain, yet he refuses to slow down or rest—even when I try to get him to relax in your lap."

Maa's laughter rang warm and comforting.

"Ah, men. When they're young, they'll run endlessly for a girl's love.

Now, Atharva runs tirelessly for his daughter's love."

Erica leaned closer, gently taking Maa's hand and resting her head on her shoulder.

"I feel so at peace here with you, Maa. Would it be alright if I stayed... if I shared the rest of my life with you?"

Maa's eyes softened, her voice tender as she replied, "Erica, you are always welcome.

You're already part of this family's love."

But Erica hesitated, her voice heavy with guilt. "Maa, I carry this weight... I feel as though I left Atharva when he needed me the most."

Maa's brows knit together in curiosity. "What happened, dear?"

Erica sighed, her heart aching as she began. "During our joint training exercises, Atharva was placed under suspension in the Air Force.

I left him... without giving him any answers. He loved me so deeply, and yet, I walked away. I never stopped to consider how much it hurt him." She paused, her voice trembling. "My unit from Ireland didn't approve of him. They even tried to sabotage his reputation. On the very last day of his suspension, I found an old letter Shruthi had written to him. I couldn't bear what it stirred inside me.

I scribbled a small note – 'Please take care' – and then walked away without ever looking back."

Maa listened quietly, her eyes filled with understanding. She placed a comforting hand on Erica's.

"You know, my dear, everything in life happens for a reason. Sometimes, the storms we face lead us to the calm we need most."

She smiled gently. "Since then, Atharva has found love in Sana, and she has brought a new light into his life. Love always finds its way when the time is right.

It's never too late to find love again, Erica. Love has its own destiny; one that's beyond any plans or fears we might have."

Erica's eyes brimmed with tears, her heart simultaneously aching and healing. In that moment, she realised that love wasn't just about timing—it was about courage, forgiveness, and the willingness to try again.

♥

Chapter Thirty-Five

Atharva gently lifted Sana into his arms, handling her with the utmost care as he made his way towards the car, his escorts quietly accompanying them.

As they approached, Atharva caught sight of Veeru at the car window, trying to give a casual, friendly salute. Atharva smiled and gestured, inviting him in.

"Hope you're doing well, Captain," Veeru greeted as he got in.

Atharva nodded, "I'm doing well." The two of them spoke about work, updating each other on recent happenings.

After a while, Atharva leaned back, adjusting his seat to get comfortable and soon drifted into a deep sleep.

In his dreams, he found himself walking into an old, familiar scene – a classroom he had seen in other dreams before.

It was strange yet oddly comforting, as though he had once been part of that world.

Last time, he had seen Shruthi here. Now, he took a seat, scanning the room until his gaze settled on a young girl approaching him.

She had a distinct, unique smile that held a hint of curiosity. As she got closer, she asked with a playful look, "So, is your narcissistic disorder cured?".

There she was—Manya, the girl from the City of Passes. Memories rushed back to him like a flood.

He remembered her laugh, the way she moved with such lightness, and the spark in her eyes that could warm the coldest mountain day.

"How are you, Manya?" he asked softly, feeling a wave of nostalgia settle over him.

Before she could respond, a man dressed in black appeared out of nowhere, swiftly pulling Manya up from the bench and whisking her away into the misty, snow-laden streets.

Atharva blinked, trying to catch a glimpse of the stranger, but his face remained hidden in the shadows.

Yet, somehow, Atharva felt he understood what Manya had been trying to tell him—something unspoken, yet lingering between them.

Maya was an orphan, he remembered, raised by the rugged beauty of Leh itself.

She was more than just a girl from the mountains; she was the heart of Leh—joyful, generous, and remarkably talented.

She had spent her life teaching the locals their own culture, sharing the intricate traditional dances, and passing down the vibrant customs of the region to each new generation.

Her spirit was contagious, and her resilience was boundless.

Atharva's thoughts drifted to the early days of his Air Force career when he and Veeru had been stationed in Leh.

It was a challenging assignment, one that demanded both mental and physical toughness.

The harsh climate, the high-altitude terrain, and the endless drills—all of it had been gruelling, but there was also something magical about the place that had seeped into his soul.

Manya looked at Veeru, her dark eyes sparkling with curiosity, and gave him that signature smile – warm, welcoming, and slightly mischievous.

"Are you here to learn the steps?" she asked playfully, as if she could read his fascination in his eyes.

And so it began.

Over the next few weeks, Veeru found every excuse to be near her, learning not just the dance steps she loved to teach but the spirit behind them.

Together, they'd walk the narrow, winding paths of Leh. Veeru was entranced by the tales Maya would spin about her childhood, her love for her people, and the way she saw the world.

She was everything he wasn't—free, spirited, and unrestrained, like a stream cutting through the mountains with an elegance that couldn't be contained.

And as much as he tried to remain composed, she melted his defences, one laugh, one glance at a time.

Manya, too, had begun to feel something stir within her.

She admired Veeru's quiet strength, the way he held himself with honour and dedication, the subtle softness in his gaze that only she could see.

In him, she found someone who was both steady and passionate, a contrast that made her feel safe yet alive.

One chilly evening, they found themselves walking along a high mountain ridge, the stars spilling across the inky sky above them.

The town below was silent. The only sounds were their hushed voices and the crunch of snow underfoot.

Manya stopped, leaning over the edge to look out at the valley stretching below.

Veeru watched her in silence, captivated by the way the moonlight painted her face, illuminating her features as if she were carved from the mountain itself.

"Why do you look at me like that?" she asked softly, catching him in his silent reverie.

"Because," he said, his voice barely more than a whisper, "you make me feel like I belong here, like I belong to these mountains and these stars, just by being here with you."

Manya's eyes softened as she looked at him, and before she knew it, she had reached out, her gloved hand resting on his cheek.

There was no need for words as they stood together, wrapped in the silence and the stars.

In that moment, Leh, with its vastness and majesty, faded into the background.

All that remained was the space between them, a quiet understanding, a love that grew unspoken.

As winter turns to spring, their love deepens.

They spent their days exploring hidden trails, sharing stories under the open sky, and teaching each other their own ways of seeing the world.

Veeru learned to dance, much to Manya's amusement. His movements were clumsy but endearing, while she marvelled at the discipline and purpose that filled his life.

She taught him the rhythms of Leh, and he showed her a life of duty and honour, a life that had once felt foreign but was now becoming her own.

But as the seasons changed, so did their circumstances.

Veeru's time in Leh was drawing to a close, and the looming knowledge of his departure hung between them, casting a shadow over their days.

They both knew that words couldn't change their fate, yet every stolen glance, every touch, every laugh shared under the fading winter skies felt like a quiet promise.

On their last night together, they returned to the ridge where they had first confessed their love, watching the sun dip behind the mountains in hues of fiery orange and purple.

Veeru held her hand tightly, committing to memory the feeling of her fingers intertwined with his, the warmth of her presence against the cold.

Neither of them spoke, knowing that words would only make it harder to say goodbye.

As the last light faded from the sky, Maya looked up at him, her smile brave but her eyes glistening.

"Promise me you'll return," she whispered, her voice trembling with hope.

Veeru pressed his forehead to hers, his own heart aching at the thought of leaving her behind.

"I promise," he said, his voice thick with emotion. "The mountains might separate us, but I'll always carry you with me. You're a part of me now, Manya."

They shared a final, tender kiss under the blanket of stars, knowing that while distance would come between them, their love would always belong to the mountains of Leh, forever etched into the heart of the City of Passes.

The very next day, the news of a landslide swept through Leh like a cold gust of wind, disrupting plans and sowing worry across the base.

Veeru, who was set to return, had his travel delayed by three days, giving him a rare pause to catch his breath.

Atharva, however, went back to his post without a second thought. To him, the landslide was just another obstacle, something to avoid and overcome.

Even as he acknowledged the beauty of Leh's peaks and valleys, he rarely felt attached to anything or anyone in the way that others seemed to.

But Atharva was vaguely aware of Manya's presence on the same route that morning.

She was travelling through the affected area, her colourful shawl a small dot moving against the vast, rugged landscape.

He saw her from his jeep as he drove with his usual air of confidence, never once breaking his determined expression.

His heart beat only for success, for the next goal to be conquered.

Warnings and risks were considerations he calculated for himself, but when it came to others, he dismissed them as unimportant, as obstacles on his own path.

He could have stopped. He could have called out to Manya, told her about the danger, but he didn't. At that moment, he dismissed her presence, thinking only of his own mission.

She was, after all, Veeru's concern, not his. And so, with a sense of indifference, Atharva continued on.

As he approached the checkpoint, a deafening rumble echoed through the mountains, a low roar that shook the ground beneath him.

Atharva's eyes widened, and he instinctively looked back, a chill creeping over him as he remembered Manya's figure moving through that same path.

Thick clouds of dust and debris rolled down the hillside, obscuring his view entirely.

The sound of boulders crashing, earth crumbling—it was a chaotic symphony of destruction.

At that moment, something inside Atharva shifted. His heart raced, pounding harder with each step as he stumbled from his jeep, the dust and smoke clouding his vision.

He felt a pang of fear—not for himself, but for someone else. The realisation was strange, uncomfortable, but undeniable.

Manya. She was on that path, the same one now buried under tonnes of rock and debris.

For the first time in as long as he could remember, he was terrified for someone other than himself.

"Please... let her be okay," he whispered, the words barely escaping his lips as he ran towards the site of the landslide, tripping over stones, blinded by the thick haze that enveloped him.

It was as though the mountains themselves were collapsing around him, the dust stinging his eyes, blurring his vision.

But he kept going, his desperation pushing him forward even as his body ached with exhaustion.

The dust finally began to settle, and his eyes searched frantically for any sign of her.

Instead, he saw nothing but debris, the landscape forever altered by the landslide's force.

In the eerie silence that followed, Atharva felt his stomach sink. He could almost see Manya's bright shawl in his mind's eye, now buried beneath the weight of the mountains.

As the dust rose, a feeling of helplessness surged within him, cutting through the shell of self-importance he had built over the years.

For once, he didn't feel invincible; he didn't feel above the world around him. He felt powerless, human, struck by the raw finality of nature's force.

Manya, the vibrant, spirited girl who had shown him kindness despite his flaws, might be gone, and he had done nothing to prevent it.

The realisation cut deeper than he could have imagined, prying open a part of his heart he had long kept shut.

His own narcissism, his callous disregard for the people around him, had finally come back to haunt him.

He was suddenly aware of how little he had truly seen Manya, Veeru, or anyone who had crossed his path with genuine warmth and care.

In the silence that followed, Atharva fell to his knees, staring blankly at the rubble, feeling the weight of his choices pressing down on him like the mountain's fallen stones.

His narcissism had shielded him from vulnerability and empathy, but now it left him hollow, a man haunted by his own failings.

He could almost hear Manya's laughter, her gentle voice, asking him why he sought validation in ways that left others behind.

He sat there, consumed by regret, a sense of loss, and shame swelling in his chest.

This time, there was no one to recognise him, no victory to claim. The mountains had taken something he couldn't win back, something that his ambition and pride could never replace.

And as the sun dipped lower, casting long shadows over the wreckage, Atharva finally understood the weight of his choices, the depth of his selfishness.

The silence of the mountains felt like judgement – a heavy, unyielding reminder of what he had lost and would never regain.

Suddenly, Atharva felt a hand on his shoulder, gently shaking him. He blinked, his vision adjusting to the dim light of the car's interior, and found himself looking up at Veeru, whose face was marked with concern.

"Hey, wake up," Veeru said softly, studying his friend's pale expression. "Are you okay? You were talking in your sleep."

Atharva sat up slowly, his heart still racing, his mind hazy from the intensity of the dream. The memory of the landslide, of Manya lost to the mountains, still clung to him like a ghost.

He looked at Veeru, his chest tight with a familiar pang of regret. "I could have stopped it… I could have warned her," he murmured, his voice rough. "But I didn't.

I didn't care enough until it was too late."

Veeru furrowed his brow, confusion and worry flickering across his face. "What are you talking about? Stopped what? Manya…? Atharva, it was just a dream." Veeru's expression softened as he added, "Come back to the present, buddy.

Sana's getting hungry, and we're almost at the camp."

Atharva let Veeru's words sink in, the fog of the past slowly lifting from his mind.

It had been a dream—a vivid, haunting reminder of a chapter he thought he'd buried.

The weight of Manya's memory, the realisation of his own selfishness, still lingered, but he was here, in the present, and life had given him another chance to learn, to be better.

♥

Chapter Thirty-Six

The quiet of Atharva's office was broken by a hesitant knock at the door.

He glanced up from his papers, expecting a soldier or an assistant, but the sight that met his eyes left him momentarily frozen.

Erica stood in the doorway, her face a mixture of nervousness and determination.

"Erica," Atharva said softly, standing as if to greet her formally. "What brings you here?"

She stepped inside, closing the door behind her, her gaze fixed on him. "Atharva," she began, her voice fragile yet resolute. Can we talk for a while?"

"Of course," he said, gesturing for her to sit. He could sense the weight of something unsaid in her demeanour.

Erica sat across from him, her fingers fidgeting with the edge of her scarf. "I've been thinking... about us," she started, looking at him directly now.

"I shouldn't have left you.

Back then, when I found that letter from Shruthi in your bag..." Her voice trailed off, but her words hung in the air like a cloud threatening rain.

Atharva's expression softened.

He leaned back slightly, exhaling as a faint smile touched his lips.

"It's okay, Erica," he said gently.

"Life had a different plan for us," he paused, then added, almost to himself, "Misunderstandings are the silent chasms between hearts, born not from words unspoken, but from truths unheard."

Erica blinked; her throat tightened at the calm acceptance in his voice.

"Did you ever really love me?" she asked, her words fragile, like a feather drifting on uncertain air.

"Yes," Atharva answered without hesitation.

His gaze held hers, steady, genuine, but tinged with a feeling of sorrow he couldn't quite hide.

Her voice dropped to a whisper. "Do you still love me?"

Atharva didn't respond immediately.

His silence was louder than any words he might have spoken.

Erica studied his face, searching for an answer in his eyes, but they gave nothing away.

After a moment, she forced a small, resigned smile.

"Alright, Atharva," she said, her voice breaking slightly. "I think it's time for me to leave."

Mithra and I will head back to my country."

Erica's lips quivered, and she looked away, trying to gather herself.

When she turned back to him, tears glistened in her eyes. "Mithra," she repeated softly, "is your boy, Atharva.*Our son.*" Her voice cracked as the words spilled out, releasing the weight she had carried for so long.

"He's our child, Atharva. Sana's brother."

Atharva's world stopped.

He stared at her, his mind struggling to process what she had just said. "Our... son?" he repeated, his voice barely a whisper.

Erica nodded, her tears flowing freely now. "Yes. He's ours. I wanted to tell you before, but I...I thought there was someone else in your life. I thought you had moved on."

Atharva's chest tightened, a wave of emotions crashing over him—shock, regret, and an overwhelming ache for all the time he had lost.

Tears welled up in his eyes as he rose from his chair, crossing the small distance between them.

Without thinking, he wrapped his arms around her, holding her tightly as sobs wracked his body.

"I didn't know," he whispered, his voice trembling. "Erica... I didn't know."

She buried her face in his shoulder, her own sobs muffled against him. "I thought I was doing the right thing.

I didn't want to complicate your life."

Atharva pulled back slightly, looking into her tear-streaked face.

"You should have told me," he said, his voice breaking. "I had a right to know... about him, about us."

"I know," Erica admitted, her voice barely audible. "I know."

For a moment, they simply held each other, their shared grief and longing filling the space between them.

♥

Chapter Thirty-Seven

"Atharva," she began, her voice trembling, "it was so difficult to raise Mithra without a father.

I was ready to take on the blame society threw at me, but Mithra—a baby, so innocent—was blamed too, for no fault of his own." Her voice cracked, and she buried her face in his chest.

"Why? Why do children, who haven't even seen the world, have to face such cruelty? Why are they punished for mistakes they didn't make? Mithra suffered before he even came into this world, and it breaks my heart to think of everything he endured."

Atharva wrapped his arms around her, his chest tightening as he listened.

Erica continued, her words spilling out in a torrent.

"Why do parents let their ego and pride tear apart their children's lives? Mithra, barely able to speak, was forced to answer for things he didn't understand.

At carnivals, at church, at school, he was always so alone.

There was no father to hold his hand in crowded places, to carry him when he was tired, or to pick him up from school.

No one to guide him when he was confused or to scold him when he made mistakes."

Her voice broke into a whisper as she choked back more tears.

"Atharva, I'm so sorry.

I thought I could manage, but Mithra bore the brunt of our mistakes.

He was taunted at school for not having a last name. He cried because of the gossip his classmates spread about him.

Children shouldn't have to answer for the failings of their parents. But because of our ego, because of our desires, our son was left to fend for himself." Erica's hands gripped his shirt tightly.

"I worked hard, Atharva, balancing everything for Mithra. But I didn't have anyone to lean on, no one to help when I needed rest. It was exhausting, both physically and emotionally.

I know it was my mistake to leave you back then, but Mithra paid the price. He avoided birthday parties and social gatherings because he was tired of being questioned.

The knowledge of his lineage, his ancestry—things a father naturally passes down.

Fathers often embody resilience, determination, and a sense of unwavering work ethic.

Mithra didn't have that figure to look up to, to emulate."

She paused, her tears streaming freely now.

"He missed having someone who would stand in line for hours, even in freezing cold, just to get him his favourite book on the very first day of its release."

Someone who would make him feel like he mattered more than anything else in the world."

She took a deep, shuddering breath, her voice gaining a quiet strength.

"Atharva, I came to this decision not just for me.

Sana needs a mother, and Mithra needs a father.

While the world is busy tearing marriages apart, let's be the ones who save ours—for our kids." Her tear-streaked face tilted up to meet his gaze.

"I want you to give Mithra the same love you've given Sana.

He doesn't know you're his father, and I don't want him to hate you when he finds out.

I want him to feel that love naturally, to discover it himself, and to grow into someone who would move mountains for his father." She placed a trembling hand on his chest.

"Show him that love, Atharva. Be the father he deserves, the one I know you can be. Let's be the family our children need.

Let's show them and the world what love can achieve."

Erica's voice quivered as she spoke, her tears falling freely, her emotions raw and unguarded."

"Mithra... he became an introvert for a reason," she began, her gaze distant as if reliving the pain of her son's silent struggles. "He never had the voice to turn around and say,

'My father will come and stand up for me if you trouble me.'

Instead, he just accepted everything—the teasing, the questions, the loneliness—as if it was all he deserved. Atharva, I don't know how deeply this has affected him, but I can feel it.

He's yearning for a father, for a fighter in his corner, someone to show him how to stand tall."

Her voice cracked as she continued, her anguish seeping into her words.

"I remember the day he refused to write his name on his books. He didn't want to, Atharva.

He didn't have a second name he was proud to claim.

He should be able to write *Mithra Atharva* in his class books and exams with pride, not with hesitation or shame."

Erica's sobs deepened, her hands trembling as she wiped her cheeks. "He regrets not having surprises, no one to pop up with a toy car just to see him smile. He never asked anyone for anything because he didn't feel he had the right.

But I want that to change. I want you to take him out, teach him how to play football, and how to ride a bicycle.

I want him to experience what it feels like to have a father," she tried to laugh through her tears, her words broken but heartfelt.

"You know, Atharva, I thought you'd see yourself in Mithra's eyes. He has so much of you in him.

He sneezes like you—those unstoppable fits that make everyone laugh—and even pauses when he talks, just like you do. It's uncanny… and it's beautiful."

Atharva pulled her closer, holding her tightly as she continued to cry. His heart ached at her words, but he couldn't stop a small smile from forming.

"I carried the burden of being judged, Atharva," Erica admitted, her voice barely above a whisper.

"People questioned my character, my decisions, and I had no one to defend me.

But my work—it became my escape.

It gave me a purpose and a sliver of respect in a world that wanted to tear me down." She looked up at him, her eyes pleading.

"We might act like we're independent, like we don't need anyone.

But if society keeps downsizing marriages in the name of freedom, what will happen to the next generation?"

Atharva's chest tightened at her words, and he gently wiped away her tears.

"Erica," he said softly, "Maa used to always tell me, *'You've done nothing wrong, so why are you suffering?'* And now, hearing all of this, I realise my loved ones—both you and Mithra—were struggling, hurting, far away from my sight.

I should have been there, Erica. For you. For him."

Erica buried her face in his chest, her sobs quietening as his arms wrapped around her, steady and sure."

Erica turned to Atharva, her eyes glinting with playful curiosity. "Can I have your wallet for a moment?" she asked.

Atharva raised an eyebrow, a smirk tugging at the corners of his lips. "Why?" he asked, his tone light yet intrigued.

"No reason. Just give it to me," she insisted, holding out her hand.

With a slight shrug, Atharva handed it over, watching as she flipped it open with a deliberate slowness.

She paused when she found an old photograph tucked inside.

Her eyes softened as she held up the picture of Shruthi.

"She's beautiful," Erica murmured, her voice carrying a blend of admiration and a touch of wistfulness.

She looked up at Atharva, her expression warm.

"Alright, let's make it a large family—with all of us together," she said, her smile gently teasing yet heartfelt.

Atharva's fingers, which had been resting lightly on the edge of the wallet, slowly loosened their grip.

It was the same feeling that washed over him the first time he saw Erica—the quiet surrender of control, a moment where everything felt natural, as if it was always meant to be.

In that moment, they both felt the weight of their shared pain and the unspoken promise to mend what was broken—not for themselves, but for Mithra and the love they both carried for him.

♥

Chapter Thirty-Eight

The house buzzed with excitement as Maa announced the preparations for Sri Krishna Janmashtami.

This year, Erica was entrusted with organising the festival, her grace and charm promising to make it unforgettable.

Draped elegantly in a dark-contrast saree that highlighted her blonde hair and striking blue eyes, she exuded an aura of timeless beauty.

The familiar scent she wore lingered in the air, a subtle reminder of her presence.

As the sun dipped below the horizon, Erica carefully dressed little Sana and Mithra in matching traditional outfits that echoed her saree's hues.

Their giggles filled the room as she patiently helped them prepare for the festivities.

Together, they carried small pots of coloured paste to the entrance, ready to recreate baby Krishna's mischievous footsteps.

With gentle guidance, Erica helped the girls dip their tiny feet into the paste, laughter bubbling as they left delicate prints leading from the door to the lawn.

The soft glow of countless diyas bathed the scene in warmth as Atharva entered, dressed immaculately in festive attire.

From the doorway, his eyes found Erica, who stood illuminated in the golden light.

She glanced up, caught his gaze, and raised a playful eyebrow.

Atharva smirked and gestured that he too would join in by colouring his feet and leaving oversized prints.

"No, no, no, Atharva!" Erica protested silently with her expressive eyes, shaking her head in mock disapproval.

But Atharva, ever the tease, mimed an exaggerated step forward, making her laugh despite herself.

With a sly grin, he signalled that he'd stop only if she agreed to a kiss.

Erica sighed, exasperated but charmed, and reluctantly walked towards him.

She stood on tiptoe, her cheeks flushed, and offered him a piece of sweet as a distraction before planting a quick kiss on his lips.

Before Atharva could react, she turned to rush away, but he was quicker.

Catching her wrist, he pulled her gently back toward him. His eyes softened as he leaned in, giving her a slow, lingering kiss.

A warm smile spread across his face as their eyes met.

Erica, flustered but smiling herself, wriggled free and darted toward the kitchen, her laughter trailing behind her.

♥

Chapter Thirty-Nine

Atharva sighed, setting down his papers as he announced, "I have to leave for Leh tomorrow morning for an urgent exercise MOU.

The weather's brutal this time of year."

Erica, her blue eyes filled with curiosity and concern, approached him quietly. In a soft whisper, she asked, "Is it really work? If it is, I want to come with you."

Atharva smiled at her tenderly, brushing a strand of hair from her face. "It's important, yes, but it won't take long.

Once it's done, we'll have plenty of time to spend together."

Sana overheard their conversation but didn't react. Knowing her school holidays were over, she quietly accepted that this wasn't her adventure to join.

The next morning, Atharva and Erica flew to Leh, the icy winds biting at their faces as they landed. The world was blanketed in snow, silent and serene.

However, upon arrival, they learned that the exercise had been postponed for two days due to avalanches.

What initially seemed like a delay turned into a gift—time for just the two of them.

Away from the strict protocols of the Air Force, they retreated to a quieter part of Leh where they could simply enjoy each other's company.

As they walked the deserted, snow-laden roads hand in hand, the world around them seemed to disappear.

The crisp air, the crunch of snow beneath their boots, and the warmth of their love painted a picture of peace.

Stolen kisses and shared laughter filled their moments.

"This feels like home," Erica whispered one evening, her breath visible in the cold air.

Atharva smiled, enchanted by her words and the glow in her eyes.

But as they walked, Erica wandered towards the edge of a frozen stream, mesmerised by its crystalline surface.

Atharva, distracted for a moment, suddenly realised the danger. His heart dropped as he saw her stepping onto the ice.

"Erica! Stop! It's a flowing stream—it's dangerous!" he shouted, his voice breaking through the stillness.

But Erica, with her ears covered against the biting cold, didn't hear him. The fragile ice gave way beneath her, and she plunged into the freezing water.

"Erica!" Atharva screamed, sprinting to the edge.

He saw her beneath the ice, her movements slowing as the icy water gripped her. Desperation surged through him as he reached into the freezing stream, grabbing her jacket.

She was caught against a rock, the current pulling her deeper.

"Hold on, Erica!" he yelled, his voice trembling with fear.

With all his strength, he pulled at her jacket, his own body numb from the cold.

The ice creaked ominously beneath him, threatening to break further, but he didn't stop.

Finally, with one last pull, he freed her and dragged her to the bank.

Her body was limp, her lips blue. "Erica, wake up! Please!" he cried, rubbing her hands, her face, doing anything to bring warmth back to her.

But there was no response.

He carried her to their car, his hands shaking as he tried to start the engine.

The battery was dead – an oversight in the relentless cold.

Frantically scanning his surroundings, Atharva's eyes locked onto a yellow board gliding closer through the misty distance. Relief mingled with urgency as the vehicle approached, and as it came to a halt, a man stepped out.

"Sir, how are you?" the man asked, his voice familiar yet muffled by the layers covering him.

Atharva froze, his breath catching.

Peering through the man's scarf-wrapped face, recognition struck like lightning – it was the taxi driver from the airport.

Memories flooded his mind, and in an instant, he connected the dots.

This man wasn't just a stranger; he was Shiru's father, the same man Atharva had met briefly when he went to see Shiru at his college.

The driver's concerned voice broke through Atharva's racing thoughts. "Are you okay?"

Atharva didn't respond with words – he couldn't. His eyes, filled with desperation and the weight of the situation, spoke volumes.

Without delay, he gestured towards Erica, unconscious and barely breathing.

Understanding the silent plea, the driver sprang into action. He opened the car door, carefully pulling Erica inside.

Then, climbing into the driver's seat, he handed his phone to Atharva.

"Call the nearest military hospital," he instructed firmly, turning the ignition with urgency.

As the car sped off, Atharva's thoughts swirled in a chaotic blend of gratitude and reflection. *Good deeds never truly leave us,* he thought.

They stay hidden in the shadows of our lives, only to emerge when we stand at the edge of our greatest trials.

God never abandons the righteous. He tests us, pushing us to the very limits of our endurance.

Yet, when we are on the brink, He always sends help—sometimes in the most unexpected form.

Looking at the driver, Atharva felt the weight of divine intervention.

Fate, it seemed, was working through the hands of this man.

With the taxi's help, they called the Air Force for support, and Erica was rushed to the nearest military hospital.

Atharva sat by her side, his heart breaking with each passing second.

The doctors worked tirelessly, but the freezing water had taken its toll.

Erica's nerves were damaged beyond repair, and her body couldn't recover.

When the doctor finally stepped into the room, his face bore the weight of the news he carried.

The words hit Atharva like a hammer to the chest. Erica was no more.

In the quiet stillness of the hospital room, Atharva sat beside her, clutching her lifeless hand in his trembling grip.

Tears streamed down his face, unchecked and unrelenting.

"You gave me everything," he whispered, his voice breaking with raw emotion. "Even in your last moments, you gave me love."

In his mind, a storm of grief raged. *Erica, you were the love of my life—the infinite sea of my existence.*

Every drop of your love filled my soul with eternity. Please, just grant me one last wish—come back to me.

Your breath gave life to everything it touched, but now, without you, I can't even breathe. If I could live my life remembering your love, I'd carry pride in my heart forever.

But now, your absence is suffocating me.

He swallowed hard, his voice trapped in the aching hollow of his chest. *How can I tell the world of this pain when my voice is bound by agony? My tears are for you, Erica.*

Every dream I ever had with you has vanished like a fleeting cloud. Every memory we made is now just a patchwork to fill the gaping emptiness inside me.

I have no more tears to cry for you, Erica—only this final prayer, this desperate plea: come back to me.

What is this feeling, this ache that questions even the heavens? What is this God who allows love to linger yet leaves it hollow? My light, my guiding star, is gone.

Her shadow, once a constant presence, has vanished. The voice that used to call my name with such warmth has fallen silent.

It's as if the rhythm of life has abandoned its own song.

Without you, the sky feels like a cruel illusion, and the earth beneath my feet turns to thorns.

Is this a nightmare, or is it the vivid agony of reality painting my world in unbearable shades of sorrow? You entered my life without introduction, stealing my breath with just a glance.

Why this silence now?

I can't bear it—this void, this loneliness—it's too much to carry on my own.

Hours later, Atharva made the long journey home, Erica's body beside him.

The weight of her absence was suffocating, pressing against his chest with each breath he struggled to take.

The air around him felt heavier, colder, as if the world itself mourned her loss.

After completing her final rites, Atharva knelt before Sana and Mithra, his hands resting gently on their small shoulders.

"Sana," he whispered gently, "from now on, you'll be Erica for Mithra.

You must care for him, as she would have."

She wrapped her small arms around Mithra, holding him close, as though her embrace could shield him from the pain that consumed him.

That night, even in her sleep, she never let go of his hand, as if afraid he might slip further into the shadows of his grief.

Mithra, lost in a storm of anguish, struggled to bear the crashing waves of his mother's absence.

It was a pain he couldn't comprehend, one too profound for words.

For the first time, and perhaps the last, he faced a sorrow that left him walking in silence, unable to escape the truth of his loss.

Sana watched him, her heart aching with a quiet determination.

She prayed fervently to God, her innocent heart pleading, *"Even the fish sink to the bottom, and the most beautiful flowers are touched by bees—everything happens under Your order.*

Please give Mithra hope for tomorrow.

Pull him forward, God, and brighten his life. Just as a sculptor shapes a stone into something beautiful through relentless strikes, let this pain mould him into something extraordinary.

Let me be his mother now, loving and protecting him more than anyone else. Guide him, and in turn, guide me too."

In the days that followed, Sana became his anchor. She shielded him with a love that mirrored Erica's, a fierce and tender devotion that knew no bounds.

Bit by bit, she guided him not with words, but with her unwavering presence, becoming both his protector and his light in the darkness.

Atharva watched them, his heart heavy yet comforted.

He realised that family wasn't just about being together every day. It was a bond forged by blood and love, unbreakable even in the face of loss.

And though Erica was gone, her love lived on—in the laughter of Sana and Mithra, in their unshakeable bond, and in the memories that Atharva carried with him, etched forever in his soul.

The End.♥

No matter how harshly life strikes, it is always about finding the strength to rise again and face the sun, like the rebirth of a new dawn.

Just as the sun cannot dim forever, the darkness cannot linger indefinitely.

It is transient, a fleeting shadow.

The key lies within us – to gather the courage to pull ourselves through the pain, to endure the storms, and to embrace the promise of light that always follows.

Dear readers, kindly sign here as a heartfelt pledge to release the weight of the past, embrace the journey ahead, and dedicate yourself to crafting a brighter and more fulfilling future.